Bound in Crystal

Narisha Rajnandan

Part One
City of the Gods

I dedicate this book to
Troy & all the MBBO

Thank you for your inspiration and
support.

Odeya is a young beautiful Guardian who was born and raised in a world called Eradonis. Unaware of her true power, she returns to her birthplace, looking for answers. Destiny, however, has other plans, taking her down a dark path to find a mysterious Black Rose. Odeya is plunged into a mythical world run by two powerful Gods, determined to control her fate. Will she discover her power and find the rose or will it destroy her?

Chapter One

A silhouetted figure emerged from the path in the misty morning. Sunlight penetrated the forest, brightened the cobblestone trail leading to an enchanted temple in Aradeya Forest. The temple, lost for eons in time but recently discovered, had been built in honour of the powerful sorceress Lavaria. She lived long before humans walked the Earth, before darkness destroyed the mortal world but these are stories lost in history, legends that became myths with only her magic living on to protect the forest.

The figure stood silently for a moment, near a broken pillar staring at the wooded door. The temple was known for its powerful and rare magic, many spells were performed here but it lost all its magic the moment the Priestess of the Silver Star, vanished without a trace many many years ago. The forest has now changed and also seems to be effected by a strange darkness that was slowly taking over.

The figure stepped closer towards the wooded door but hesitating, pondering if she should proceed. Taking a deep breath, she courageously placed her quivered hand on the faded symbol.

I, Odeya. Call upon the Ancients to grant me access to this great Temple.
Let you magic flow within me to unseal.
Let me beyond this door.

Bands of fire outlined strong tapered fingers, meeting at the bottom of her palm and the door swung opened. She stepped in but the Temple was in darkness. She summoned three light orbs. They were bright enough to light up the entire Temple hall way. "that's much better!" whispered Odeya.

She focused on her surroundings, everything was old and dull. She remembered from her childhood that the pillars had magical blue vines. The vines and the beautiful red leaves had all dried. The glistening red marble floor no longer had its brilliant shine. There were no fire orbs to be seen, that use to light up the sky roof every full moon. She spent her first 7 years in this Temple. Mystified by all of its enchantment. Now it was all dull and gloomy.

She stood near the ancient bowl that stood in top of a white pedestal, but the mystic red liquid had dried up. The only thing that was left, was the dried flower. The magic that kept the flower alive had faded to nothing. She picked up the gem-like flower but it crumbled into ash, it had lost its composure and essences which permeated the air.

She dusted the ash onto the floor and slowly lowered her hood revealing her silver white hair. She had a mysterious look of unearthly beauty and her stormy silver eyes could reveal many secrets. Odeya was uneasy; she had to know what happened to this beautiful Temple. What had happened to Haniel? Why had she disappeared wondered Odeya. Haniel was a magic priestess of the Silver Star, a rare magic as only a few can harness its power from the stars.

Being raised by a priestess had some benefits for Odeya. Learning about the mysteries and magic of this world at a young age; but at times she longed for a life away from the Temple. Odeya had just completed her advanced training, away from the temple, when she heard the news about Haniel's disappearance. She was devastated.

Drained from her long travels back to the temple, she walked passed the white marble statues of the Gods Odeya knew nothing about their legends or the history of this land. She turned to look at the statues once more hoping to find some answers in them.

She eventually breaks away from the though and goes into Haniel's private quarters. She could use some sleep but this wasn't the best place. She felt a chill wind through a broken window. When she stepped closer towards the window she could see a storm brewing in the distance. Storms are rare in this part of the forest she heard. She could feel its power, as if the storm was summoned by the Gods. Its was one of her gifts to sense magic in mortals or in the atmosphere.

Her memory of this place felt like a distance dream which was now faded. Odeya realized she could not stay here. Something wasn't right about this place. She needed answers to her troubled visions and only Haniel could help. Somehow Odeya instincts told her Haniels disappearance is linked to the Black Rose. She heard rumours about an Ancient Black Rose. Its origins unknown. She thought of the Royal Library were she could hopefully find something that is linked to the Rose. It was one of the biggest Libraries in Arydress and it held many secrets hidden within the doors that not even the Empress knows all what's behind those doors.

"I will find you Haniel I promise" whispered Odeya.

~ *** ~

She found an enchanted black bag near a broken table as she walked into one of the store rooms hoping to get something she could use or maybe a gift for Avril but it was raided. This Temple was left abandoned for many years. Broken bottles and red dust lay scatted across the floor. She recognised the dust as fire dust which was used to make camp fires. She found an unbroken empty bottle and scooped in some of the fire dust, it glowed in the palm of her hands. She could feel the heat almost burning though. As she poured the dust into the bottle it turned black and the glow vanished.

While sealing the bottle, though she heard a faint voice and stood frozen for a moment. "Haniel?" she called out.

This Temple was build by the Ancients and she knew that strange things often happens here. "Hello! Anyone here?" she yelled out. She waited and listen for a voice that might portray a person but nothing.

Something caught her attention under the rumble, as she removed some broken wood she found an old book. As she picked it up she felt it's energy flowing thought her and strange Rune markings appeared on her right palm. It felt like some magic just bound her to the book. She took the book back to the main hall. She sensed knew that the threat has passed so it was safe enough to study the book.

Her hands caressed the cover of the book with the feel of newly-cured blue dyed leather. There was no name only a symbol which she had seen the it before while in training but never asked what it meant. Slowly opened the book but felt no magic or spell that could reveal a curse.

The pages were very old and it felt thick, it had a brownish colour but the letters were dark red as if it was written in blood. She gazed at the first printed lines:

Guardians of Villadon
Soldiers of God

Novayin Greeks
Aveileyains

Hidden Shadow
Fierce Dragon
Brutal Cerberus
Spirited Storm
Blood Assassin
Ancient Serpent Sea

Odeya tried to make sense of it but the word Shadow sounded so familiar that a vision appeared in her mind. Her visions revealed a powerful warrior chained to a stone table. Her instincts told her that this is linked to some-kind of Shadow. Most Odeya's visions were dark and patchy but she slowly tried to put the pieces together.

She turned to the next page:

Ancient Sea Dust & Mist

The most rare ingredient to find and powerful enough to summon a deadly storm on land or at sea. This can only be found in a place of the Gods. It is…

The rest of the words had been faded, Odeya could not make out the letters. Had the book lost some of it's magic she wondered. The other pages were blank, her finger ran down the pages hoping that it could reveal more but nothing happened. She decided to take the book with her so that she could restore its lost magic. She found a grey bag with red symbols. As she placed the book and the fire dust into a grey bag she had found, she heard something fall in the store room. She strap the bag across her shoulder and went to inspect. She nervously approached the store room calling out "whose there." Not knowing what to expect, she came upon a lion cub.

"Astarlin" she yelled. It was the Lion Cub that she adopted all those years ago. A gift from her birth mother. "I'm so glad to see you" she said.

"I'm so glad to see you" she said.

She kneed down to cuddle her beloved Astarlin. After so many years away she was so glad to see him. Astarlin was a rare enchantment Cub it never aged. The cub even helped the Empress to deliver messages to other Kingdoms using Royal Scrolls. Astarlin's magic was rare not even Odeya could explain and no mortal could have created this enchantment.

"maybe it's time we return to the Palace before the storm gets worse, don't you think?" She asked Astarlin. A soft roar came from the cub and she took it as a yes. She could still feel a slight chill in the air, could it be from the storm she wondered. She looked around and then noticed a mysteries red mist forming on the ground. "this can't be good" she whispered to Astarlin.

As the mist swirled around her she stood frozen. It felt like a dream. As the mist slowly covered everything Odeya started to feel claustrophobic. There was no escape. "Astarlin!" she yelled. Something was not right, everything around her was changing, she realized that she was no longer in the Temple. The floor became soft. She needed to find a way out of the mist quickly so she summoned an orb to guide her but the journey felt endless.

After a while she felt a warm breeze and the mist began to thin which was a relief. She felt sunlight on her skin as she finally emerged from the mist. A colossal gold statue of a mysterious God stood before her holding up a huge fire ball but it looked more like the sun. It never occurred to her that statue could be one of Helios, the Titan God of the Sun. "Why am I here?" she whispered. A feeling of warmth passed through her as if the Titan could sense her presence and was drawing her closer. She started to allow herself to be drawn in by the statue.

It was only at this point that she became aware that a massive Palace stood behind the statue. There was a long suspension bridge leading to the Palace. "could this be the Palace of Helios that she saw in her dreams?" she wondered. "what magic has brought me to this place?"

She listened but the only sound she heard was the howling wind. She wondered if the Titan was present in this Palace or was it build by mortals just to honour him. She had no intention of meeting a Titan or any other fearsome God but she had to know for sure. She took the first step, each square block on the gold bridge had a painting of a silver sun which was strange to her, the sun symbol was meant to be gold signifying Helios. Why was it silver, she wondered? Thick ropes held the bridge in place, it glowed when she held onto them rope but the glow disappeared the moment she let go. Columns of thin silver chain-like ropes stood on each side which gave it a unique look and style which tempted her to investigate. Gold was extremely rare in Eradonis and the discovery of a large amount of gold will make her rich but this belong to someone.

She took another step onto the gold block refocusing on her task of getting across. Although the bridge looked steady, it continued to shake with every step she took and she hated every moment of it. When she looked down at the river and realized how high above she was it sent a terrifying chill down her spine. She dared not fall into the raging water.

She let out a breath of air and processed again but the moment she looked straight ahead, a little girl stood at the end of the bridge. Odeya froze, although she looked more like a Goddess she could feel her rage. Her wings were blood red, Odeya realized that she was a Guardian of the dead but not for mortals. To her knowledge they were created by Helios to protect ancient tombs of Gods and fallen Heroes but who was she protecting she wondered. Her knowledge of magical creatures and Goddess came in useful to her.

Some strange magic has brought her to this unknown Palace, she thought of Haniel but the Priestess didn't possess so powerful magic. Odeya felt that she was not meant to be here but the only way to return home was to move forward.

The moment Odeya stepped forward an invisible force passed through her she let out a raging scream but she held her ground. It was some warning telling her to stay back and things were about the get worse when she heard a loud snap. A rope supporting the bridge had snapped. Then another loud snap above, she looked above her to see a sold red and gold rods that attached the ropes had fallen off.

The walkway below her began to buckle. "No! Please don't do this to me now" Odeya held onto the rope as the bridge broke off, and she hit the side of the cliff hard. Her entire body racked with pain and could barely hang on, eventually losing her grip. As she fell, she felt her strength weaken the moment she hit the raging water.

She managed to surface but struggled for breath. The water's current was strong and swept her away. She felt the water around her became icy and it felt as if she was drifting downstream. Then something within her began to surface, consuming her mind and body as her strength gave in and she fall unconscious.

Chapter Two

Odeya awakened, her eyes were still hazy. It took a moment for her eyes to adjust to the light. As she rolled over onto her side, to her surprise she felt soft silk sheets. She paused for a moment to take in the unfamiliar surroundings.

"Haniel!" she yelled.

She forced herself out of the bed but the moment she tried to stand, her legs felt like jelly and she collapsed onto the floor. How long was she out for? She wondered.

She held onto the bed and slowly picked herself up. As she gained strength, the first thing she noticed was that she was no longer wearing her black dress. The dress she now wore was short, Greek style with a thin double gold belt around her waist. Was it a gift from the Gods? Her boots were removed and she could see a silver sun tattoo on her right ankle. What was his intention for marking her? All these questions in her mind made her wary. As she held onto the bed she glanced around the massive room. Noticing the silver and gold pillars in a semi-circle around the bed. She hadn't seen gold sheets before and there was a sweet smell in the air, one that Odeya did not recognized. The walls were covered in artwork that stretched across the walls. It was the most beautiful artwork she had even seen. The scenes depicted looked like the Titans fighting for control.

Could it be the war with Zeus? But Odeya didn't recognize the God in any of the paintings. This was a war of a different era, one that wasn't in any of the ancient books that she had studied. She stepped closer to one of the painting, there was ancient Greek writings at the bottom. She wished she could stay and decipher the writings but she was in a foreign place.

"Hello!" she yelled.

The place was eerily quiet, as she left the room, she had to find a way out looking down a long corridor but she didn't know where to start, there must be a thousand rooms and she was not sure if this palace was safe. She slowly climbed down a few steps. There in front of her stood a crystal round table, filled with mouth-watering food. Was this another gift or it could be poisoned? The smells of the roast pork drew her close, her fingers touched the sticky sauce and she tasted it, hoping that it was not poisoned. She paused for a second, there was no pain or dizziness which was a relief. Her stomach growled as she hadn't eaten for days. Odeya broke off a chuck of meat, her fingers sank into the soft meat as she took a bite.

The sticky sauce dripped down her chin but she didn't care, she was hungry. It had a spicy honey taste which she hadn't come across in Eradonis before. A discovery she intend to find out about but not now. It felt like she hadn't eaten for days and the food was just so heavenly she could not stop eating.

Every bite was like heaven in her mouth but somehow this was all very familiar to her as if this meal was something she had in her past. She glanced at a jar filled with a blue liquid, she dare to taste it. She wiped her sticky hands and reached for the glass jar. A strong feeling of deja-vu returned. It felt like she had been here before and shared a meal with someone. Odeya was confused.

She sipped the blue liquid and she loved the taste, it felt sweet and chilled in her mouth. A refreshing drink was Ambrosia, food for the Gods. This was a strange place that she would love to explore but she had to find a way back home.

~***~

After the divine meal she enjoyed, she could not rest until she found a way out and she thought she heard a sound coming from behind a black double door which was not for from where she had her meal.

She bravely walked towards the doors and slowly opened it wondering what was awaiting behind the doors. There was silence at first, but there in front of Odeya, stood the little girl she had seen earlier, at the end of the passageway, the girl's smile brighten her heart. She turned around and headed for an open door at the other end of the room. "Wait!" said

Odeya. Odeya decided to follow the little girl. As she ran behind her. Odeya passed through a thin black liquid layer; she nervously took a small breath, discovering that the air was fresh and sweet smelling. The little girl disappeared into the shadows of the doorway.

She used her intuitive ability to sense for any traps but found none, she breathed a sigh of relief. Odeya slowly walked down a narrow passageway into another chamber. The walls were gold with strange symbols and marking. She cautiously moved towards a light which lead her into a large chamber. She walked in, and noticed her reflection on the shiny floor. The walls were covered in paintings, one of which showed a Goddess fighting some shadow. Another showed a Goddess sitting on a throne but this painting was damaged, she could not see the Goddesses face. The last painting was not very clear but she could see that the Goddess depicted again, wearing a mask and holding a black shiny box. She walked closer to eight statues in the room, all in a circle holding two swords in each hand. The swords were held in an x formation. Each blade touched the other which formed a link. It looked more like a Tomb.

Odeya realized that they were guarding a box that was floating in the centre of the circled statues. The box radiated light. A chill ran down her spine just looking at it. She could not take her eyes off this mysterious box. It was as if she was drawn to it. She had to know what was it. The box was pure black. She sensed an enchantment as she walked around the statues. The statues faced a small pool of thin black liquid into her hand and it formed a black orb. It was freezing she could not hold it must longer and dropped it to the ground and it shattered like glass and inside the orb was crystal dust.

"What am I doing? asked Odeya

Odeya looked at the dust as it glowed and covered the entire floor. The dust had also covered the eight statues, slowly easting away the stone of the statues.

"That was too easy!" said Odeya.

She walked towards the box and placed her hand on it. Nothing happened. She turned it around and found strange markings on it. She tried everything to open the box but nothing worked. Odeya decided take it with her, hoping that she could figure out how to open it later. The light inside the box began to fade when she took it away from its resting space and the room became dark.

The middle pool slowly started to glow brightening the room. She walked towards the pool and the golden orb within was the source of the light. She reached for it and she held it in her hand. The orb floats above her hand, slowly melting and forming a thin sheet like glass. Odeya looked closely, words formed in black which she reads it aloud:

A Journey To The Unknown Land
A World Beyond
Where It All Began
&
The Fabled Black Rose Will Be A Gift For Only The
Strongest

Odeya held the soft glass paper in her hand. The black ink turned red, forming a map. "This cannot be true! Does the Black rose really exist?" said Odeya.

Two Bo staffs appeared opposite each other, floating above the pool, a martial arts weapon rarely found in Eradonis. Odeya used her telekinesis to grab the staffs. A rush of energy invaded her body, a light momentarily penetrated every cell of her body as her fear disappeared like the morning dew. A calmness surrounded her. Its power made her skin tingle as the markings on her hands appear again glowing red. She examined the runes on her hand and wondered what they meant. As she pondered the meaning of her discovery, Odeya heard footsteps. Too loud and distinct to be mistaken for anything else. Odeya quickly rolled up the enchanted map and placed it in her black bag.

"She's in here!" she heard someone shout.

Odeya froze, there was only one way out of the chamber but a dark haired man blocked her path. He stood tall, dressed like an assassin but he looked more like the God of War. He was huge and getting past him will be a mission.

"You have entered a forbidden tomb and you have something what does not belong to you!" he said in a deep voice.

"Tomb? Are you the Guardian of this tomb?"

What was the force that drew her to this ancient box, wondered Odeya; was there some dark magic that the assassin was guarding she wondered this was linked to Helios?

"Do you think I will return the box without a fight!" said Odeya. The Assassin took Odeya's word as a challenge and stepped forward allowing another group of assassins to enter the room and surround her. "So you are the leader of the pack?" Her words angered him even more. He pointed his sword at her chest. "Let me guess" said Odeya. "You are Helios's personal assassin. So the Titan does know I'm here; this changes things" she said. "You are protecting this ancient box and not the map"

"Map?" he asked in confusion. Odeya knocked his blade away from her chest but he slashed viciously at her. Blood dripped from her face. Five more warriors surrounded and attacked her. Although she was outnumbered she managed to block their attacks.

Her skill matched their speed and agility but the Assassin was not impressed. A fury of energy surrounded Odeya's attackers as she blocked their attack with the Assassin's hatred building deep inside with a thunderous force but before he could strike her again she rolled over avoiding his further attack.

The red mist returned swirling around them. It suddenly appearsed to create a barrier between Odeya and her attackwes. Odeya felt herself drifting away and she found herself back at the entrance of the Aradeyin Temple. Her attackers nowhere to be seen.

"Thank God!" said Odeya.

Odeya's thoughts went immediately to her pet lion cub Asterlin. She was with him when she was whisked away. She searched for her pet but Asterlin was nowhere to be seen. Odeya ran to the door of the Temple and called Kitara. Another rare gift from her mother, a pure-white mare. So pure white it was as if the Gods created this beautiful horse. As usual, Kitara appeared after a few moments.

She mounted her horse. Glad for the familiarity of a trusted friend but she soon became distressed as she saw the assassin materialized from the mist.

She urged her horse to a gallop as they headed toward the dense forest losing her Bo staff in the panic. Fortunately, Kitara knew the way home so Odeya freed her hands, reaching deep within herself to draw upon her magical energy. She concentrated it into a sphere and cast a powerful fire bolt towards the Assassin. Odeya was hoping to slow him down but her aim was not steady and she missed him by inches. He continued his charge, determined to cripple his target.

It was difficult riding fast through a forest, avoided the trees that blocked her path which grew thick as she rode deeper into the forest. She looked back in an attempt to summon another fire bolt but Odeya seemed to have lost the Assassin. The enemy plagued her mind and she had forgotten that this forest had powerful lightning traps. Kitara normally knew how to navigate the forest but Odeya was pushing Kitara too hard. As she crossed the path of a lightning trap, running straight into it was unavoidable.

The energy force was so strong it knocked Odeya violently onto the ground leaving her stunned. Her horse disappeared into the think forest more frightened than anything. She screamed as pain shoot thought her body, she lay on the cold ground weakened, a voice from within telling her to run. Odeya held onto a tree to force herself up but the mist which was generally around, this deep in the forest, was so think she could barely see her enemy. She closed her eyes to cast a spell.

Reveal my enemy
Footsteps so silent
Let light show me
My enemy's path

The spell revealed that the Assassin was moving swiftly through the forest, straight towards her. In a panic she grabbed her dagger. The assassin, burning with rage came closer to unleash a blow to her head, to finish her faster but she gathered her remaining strength, fighting through the pain, rolled backwards to briefly escape a head-crushing death.

Deep breaths filled her lungs. Still weak from the lightning energy, she knew magic was her strength, so she cast an ancient red vine spell. The vines came from beneath the soft ground and swarmed all around the Assassin. She took the opportunity to disarm her attacker and she drove her blade into him; missing his heart by a very small margin. She could still sense danger as the assassin unleashed a growl, insane with rage, it sounded like he was suffocating on his own hatred. Feeling the blood and heat from his breath on her face as she saw her attacker's actions written on his face.

Heavy rain started pouring which brought a cold chill to her as she slowly backed away from Assassin. Something deep inside her stopped her from ending his life. Somehow she felt she knew him and that he was not an ordinary Assassin. She quickly turned away from him to make her escape. At a safe distance from the Assassin she began took for Kitara.

Her bare feet sank into the soft mushy ground. She felt the coldness on her feet with each step she took. She was a distance from the assassin which gave her time to catch her breath. The heavy rain spattered onto her skin, making her shiver once more. Her wet hair sticking onto her face as she moved.

Walking deeper into the forest, she came across a river. She hadn't been to these parts before. The assassin clearly had pushed her deep into the forest. Odeya stood at the edge of the river, shivering to the bone. She saw Kitara moving slowly through, the not far from the opposite river bank.

Odeya wanted to go to Kitara but the moment her foot touched the water, she froze, the water was unbearably icy for her to cross but she had to get to Kitara, so she pressed on.

The water level reached her waist which made it difficult to cross, deep breaths filled her lungs. Frozen from the icy water, she grabbed onto a rock forcing herself forward.

As she emerged from the river, onto a grassy bank, an arrow struck a tree above her. Astonished, Odeya turned to see the Assassin nearing the river bank, bow in hand. He was still alive.

Odeya got to her feet and ran towards the horse, her fear returned when he began his pursuit once again.

The assassin aimed another arrow, which struck Odeya's left shoulder, the pain shot through her body but that didn't stop her. She looked back for the assassin but he had vanished. She scanned around for the Assassin but there was no trace of him anywhere. She screamed as she pulled the arrow out of her shoulder. It burned her skin as it came out.

"Poison!" she said.

She dropped the arrow in fear, this was an unknown poison. This could change things for her and she only had her dagger to defend herself. With her magic bag that contained the ancient box safely around her back, she looked for Kitara; but she had disappeared again and she was hoping that the assassin hadn't killed her beloved Kitara. Odeya became desperate in her search so she closed her eyes and listen to the sounds of the forest. She was hoping to locate the assassin and Kitara. In the far distance she heard her horse but still no sign of the Assassin. Something was terribly wrong, how could he shield himself from her magic, no ordinary assassin could do that, there was something deeper, more powerful about him.

Then, to her left the Assassin appeared. He appeared consumed with rage and hatred which took her by surprise. He swung his blade but Odeya blocked his attack with just her dagger but she didn't have the strength to push back.

"You should have killed me when you had the chance!" he said.

"Wait! Why is this box so important?" she asked. "Surrender now and I will let you live" he said. She looked into his cold eyes and knew that even if she returned the box he would still kill her. She will fight till her last breath. "Not going to happen" she said.

"Then you will die today" he said. She gripped the dagger and sliced him across his chest. Blood spilled onto the ground, a loud roar escaped his lungs and he slashed at her without mercy but Odeya dodged his every attack but she wasn't fast enough. The assassin sword left a deep slash across her face resulting in blood and sweat dripping from her face. She let out a loud cry but that didn't stop the assassin. The cuts on her hand, face and a blood stained dress proved that he was determined to end her life and no mercy was shown by him.

The assassin, angered by her resistance, combined his hatred into a hard hit, as she smashed into the ground, the assassin pined her down with an invisible force. "This ends now!" he grunted. He gripped onto the bag and tossed it aside. "No!" Odeya yelled.

Before Odeya could defend herself, his blade pieced straight into her heart. Her cries of pain did not affect him, without mercy he ripped his blade out.

Her rune markings appeared glowing silver, in a state of shock he glanced at the young woman. Her markings then appeared in the air which created a shield around them.

She slipped into an unconscious state but he sensed that she was still alive which only meant one thing. She possessed power beyond normal. Her fighting skill matched his but he needed to know for sure so he dipped his finger into her blood and tasted it. "No! You are... Odeya!"

His heart sank, he had been looking for her for thousands of years and finally found her. In the mitts of despair, he took his blade and pieced the ground, created a fire circle for protection. He locked his forearm with her, as the shadow energy spiralled around their forearms, he dropped to his knees but did not dare to let go. He finally found his little sister and now will give his own life just to save her. A terrible thing he did and will not forgive himself but he couldn't have known she was his sister. The shadow energy filled every inch of her body, her beautiful silver hair turned pitched black. Ripped through his entire mortal body causing him to bleed but he was not willing to let go. He had to endure the pain even if it kills him. He was transferring his divine power into her and it also healed her wounds but it weakened him and he finally let go. It took every ounce of his strength to ensure that she could live. He fell back and the shield around them vanished, Odeya recovered but remind in a semi-sleep state. He could feel his divine light had faded as he lay on the cold ground.

"Ichiro!" he called out.

Chapter Three

Odeya awakened on the soft grass, her eyes slowly adjust to the light. As she lay on the cold ground she felt like a strange warmth within her blood like something awakening deep within her, something she could not explain. Odeya remembered the pain when the blade pieced her chest, but she could not find a wound. Had the blade pieced her? Did she imagine it all? Had she been brought back to life; she wondered.

She slowly picked herself up, glanced at her surroundings, the forest was eerie silent not an animal or bird in slight, the mist was unnatural, almost grain like, like it was being controlled by an unknown force. Odeya realized that if she stayed here any longer, it will drive her mad. A lot of unexplained magic filled these parts of the forest.

Odeya heard a faint noise from behind and she turned to investigate. To her relief it was Kitara. It brought a smile to her gloomy face. "I'm so glad you safe" she whispered. There was an unbreakable bond she shared with Kitara and couldn't bear to lose her. "We need to leave!" she said to Kitara. She examined her enchanted bag before she tied it to the saddle, the ancient box was still safely packed away. She glanced that the setting sun, she remembered rumors of a guardian wolf that stalks the forest attacking intruders not knowing if it's friend or foe. She didn't want to stick around to find out, she mounted Kitara leaving her fear behind and rode off.

~ *** ~

When she reached the boundary it was like shimmering wall of silver stars. Odeya dismounted and placed her right hand on the glowing wall. It opened up a circle allowing her to pass. She grabbed her reins and pulled Kitara through the boundary. It felt like a weight had been lifted from her shoulders but sleeping out in the open could be risky knowing that the assassin is still out there. She looked at the last fading light and in the distance you could see the wheat fields of Arydress. She's one step closer to the Royal Palace. She hoped for shelter and a decent meal when she reached there, just a simple freshly baked bread to cure her hunger.

She decided to rest for the night before she crossed the wheat fields. She found a large berry tree, with fruit known as blood berries; a very sweet fruit but it was the only thing she could eat, hunting was not the best thing right now. She quickly filled a bottle with many round berries. A protection spell was needed before she could think of making a fire or she would be exposed. She could use the moonlight as a source of energy to make the spell stronger. She learnt many spells while in training, but casting spells were not an easy task. Some powerful spells required light or darkness, but elemental spells were the hardest to summon. She thought of one that will work at night but casting might be a bit tricky. In order for it to work she required the venom from an Olakin snake, it was one of the deadliest snakes in Eradonis. One bite can cause hours of intense pain before one die.

To hunt one could be a awful task, so Odeya placed her right hand onto the ground and she drew energy from within to attracted the snake towards her. "Okay! I can do this" she whispered. She slowly took out her dagger ready to strike if anything goes wrong with her magic. Odeya could see the snake slowly sliding towards her, she then sifted her energy to control the snake. She placed the dagger onto the ground and grabbed a bottle from the bag. She wasted no time and grabbed the snake by it's head, extracting the venom using magic. She guided the poison venom into the bottle and sealed it. Odeya carefully released the snake. As she watched it slither away, it that crossed her mind that her magic had grown even more powerful with her training.

Odeya summed a light orb and went in search of Moonlight lilies which was the next ingredient she needed for the spell. While looking she noted that there was a sudden drop in temperature, she need to find the flower before she froze to death. She closed her eyes and stood for a moment slowly adsorbing everything around her. She used her senses to locate the mystic flower. She sensed one to her left, near a tree not far from where she was standing. She could see a few glowing and quickly pulls them from the ground. She noticed that the glow has not faded which was needed for the spell. She heads back to Kitara and gets to work on the spell. Odeya removed the petals and placed them around in a circle and dusted the pollen onto the petals. She picked out a leaf and five drops of the venom fall onto the first petal. A red symbol appeared. She continued with each petal and mixed the remaining pollen into the venom, still in the jar with a small twig. It slowly turned into a black liquid. She whispered a spell:

Let this be hidden from my unseen foe.
I summon the Blood symbol of binding
Come to me oh great serpent
Let your magic flow onto me
Give me immunity in this spell

She took a sip of the black liquid. It tasted like ash. She poured the remaining liquid onto the ground. Black vines from beneath her feet formed a barrier all around her. The flowers that grew had a deadly poison, none will dare to enter.

She quickly gathered some twigs to make a fire, laid it onto the ground and sprinkled some of the fire dust that she found in the Temple and it was lit in no time. Tiredness was quickly seeping in and she didn't care about her hunger or the berries any longer. She rested with her back against a tree listening to the sounds of the forest; slowly drifting off to sleep, knowing that the spell would keep her safe.

~***~

She was awakened by the warm morning sun, but her tired eyes could barely open from the lack of adequate sleep. Was it the battle that not only drained her so much but her magical energy as well she wondered. When she looked up she could see the city walls. It was a moment of absolute joy for her.

"I'm home" she said softly, just adsorbing in the moment. The weather was perfect. Clear skies with a cool breeze; it was the beginning of Spring. She closed her eyes to embrace the sunlight, she was finally home after many years of training. She stepped onto the dried vines that had served their propose. She grabbed the jar of berries and stuffed a few in her month as she gathered her all belongs and mounted Kitara.

~ *** ~

As she rode into the town, she took in the sights and smells of the crowded streets. People talked and laughed as they went about their daily routines, while children ran and played in the street. Several citizens greeted her as she passed, reminding her of how welcome she always felt whenever she was here. The years have passed but aside from folks growing older, not much else had changed. She dismounted and led her horse the rest of the way. She slowly made her way to a nearby stable and greeted the owner with a smile. "Good Morning Oresus" said Odeya.

"Odeya! Is that you? What have you done with your hair, I didn't recognize you?"

"Where have you been all these years?" Oresus asked.

"It's a crazy story" said Odeya.

"Ah! It's a perfect morning to share your story with an old friend, don't you think?"

"Maybe some other time, I feel like I just want fall flat onto a soft bed" said Odeya.

"I guess you need it, you look like just came out of the…"

"Please don't say it!" said Odeya.

"So have you heard any news about your father?" asked Odeya.

"Yes! They plan to release him in a months' time but it's been so many years" said Oresus.

Odeya's memory of Oresus was a sad one. He lost his mother at a young age and it was not long when his father was taken prisoner in Siacodia for stealing from the Royal Palace.

"I never stopped thinking about my father, it was my fault that he is in prison so how do I face him after all these years?" Oresus asked.

"I'm sure your father has forgiven you and will be glad to see you. Don't give up hope" said Odeya.

"Thank you for your kind words, much appreciated" said Oresus.

"I was wondering if you would keep Kitara for a night I will be very grateful," she asked.

"You don't need to ask," he said.

He slowly raised from his chair, walked towards the horse and unsaddled Kitara. "Thank you Oresus." Said Odeya.

"No problem." Said Oresus looking at Odeya with concern.

"Well! I should go" said Odeya.

"So where are you off to? Have you heard? There is some dark energy lurking in the in the shadows around us. Some say it came from the Sacred Lands" said Oresus.

"The Sacred Lands? That's been abandoned for many years, no one goes there anymore" said Odeya.

"Well rumors say it's linked to the Lord of Darkness"

"That doesn't sound too good but maybe I need to see it for myself to believe it" said Odeya.

"Afraid you cannot enter, The Empress has it blocked" he said.

"Well! I should get going" said Odeya still playing what Oresus said on her mind.

"Take care!" said Oresus.

They say their goodbyes and he turned towards the door which lead into the lower stables. She was also grateful for his years of a friendship. Oresus's father taught her and his son how to ride a horse when she was only ten years old. It was an enjoyable experience for the young Odeya. She learnt new things from him over the years and a good friendship had been maintained with Oresus.

~***~

She slowly strolled through the streets and in a short distance she could see trouble brewing. Soldiers were escorting a prisoner, the chains around her hands were strongly bound. Odeya watched the young woman as she walked passed but the prisoner took no notice of her, the crowd started throwing stones at the prisoner. Odeya wondered what crime she has committed. She wanted to ask one of the soldiers but they will probably not recognize her. She then noticed the Royal symbol on their armor, it was the Empress's personally group of elite soldiers, not Royal guards. Soldiers of Arydress that no one dares to mess with. They are known to be fierce in battle and never lost a war. They also have a strong will to protect those who are weak when they make their rounds throughout the city.

Odeya had known every soldier in the Palace and she knew that they will give their lives to protect the Empress. The Empress Avril is also not someone to be trifled with. She had seen Avril fight to keep her Throne. Odeya had also witnessed the hardships of Royal life.

Odeya watched them drag the woman; they were heading to Avril's Palace. She was curious but something else grabbed her attention. A mysterious figure brushed passed her and she could feel his power as it filled her veins. She glanced at him as he stopped, he turned to face her. It felt like a powerful connection; something that she could not explain. She froze when the cloaked figure stepped closer, his hood was up and she could barely see his face. "Odeya!" he whispered. His voice sounded so familiar. She stood in the middle of the streets bewildered until one of the solder bumped into her which brought her out of a daze, before she could realize what had happened. The mysterious figure vanished as if it was one of her visions. She glanced around hoping to find him but the streets were crowded and they were too busy with their daily lives to pay attention to her. She asked a few people but none had seen or heard about the mysterious figure.

~***~

The air felt heavenly when she smelled the freshly baked pies that made her mouth water. She was temped to try one, she spend a lot of time in the market as a child. It was her passion for food that drew her to this market, she loved to taste different kinds of food. She stood for a moment staring at the pies, it was pure joy to see the market once again. She had forgotten what good food tastes like but she barely had enough to buy it.

Odeya looked around the market, just enjoying the sights, sounds and smells when in the near distance she recognized a young girl. She recognized her as Tayana so she approached her through the busy streets.

"Tayana!" called Odeya.

The little girl ignored the stranger that called her name but Odeya persisted. "I am Odeya" she said.

Tayana stopped and turned around. The child's beauty reminded her of Avril, it was like she was part of the Royal line of Arydress. Her long red hair was the same length as Avril's but she was the daughter of Ayalet. Although most people in Arydress had red hair, but whenever Odeya looked into the child's beautiful hazel eyes she sense there was something unique about her.

Odeya walked closer to her and rested her hands on Tayana's shoulders. "You are all grown up, you must be six or seven years old?" Odeya asked.

"Seven! Odey. Wow I am so happy to see you. It has been so long. I always think about you. When I grow up I want to be just like you, a powerful and strong Archer" said Tayana filled with excitement.

"Hmm, your mother must be filling your head with tales of my adventures but you are too young to learn archery sweetheart" said Odeya.

Disappointed by Odeya's words. She turned her back to Odeya. Odeya could tell that she was frustrated and refused to face Odeya. Odeya seemed to let her down but Tayana could not handle a weapon that was larger than she was and anyway she would not have the strength to pull the taut string back far enough to send an arrow any further than a few inches. Odeya walked around her to face Tayana, she looked up at Odeya and gave her a smile.

"I will need your mother's approval before I can teach you anything but first you must be a little older, training is not easy" said Odeya.

"Promise?" she asked.

"Promise! So now were can I find your mother, I would love to see her." said Odeya.

An angry look crossed her face again. "She is in that stupid tavern and she is too busy to play with me" said Tayana.

"Have you tried the snow cream?" said Odeya trying to distract Tayana. "How about we get some, I bet your mother doesn't have time anymore to make you some"

"Yes! lets go! I know where it is" said Tayana excitedly.

She guided Odeya leading her across the busy street into a wooded walkway. There was a large stall, many vendors severing snow cream. It had grown popular as time passed. Snow cream was very rare in Arydress and it was quite difficult to find the ingredients to make it and it requited a unique skill to add the finishing touches.

As they approached they were greeted with a warm smile. "Good Morning! What can I get for you?" The vendor asked.

"What are the new favors?" Odeya asked.

"Well! we have spiced lemon, cheesy chocolate, honey berry and blue iced chocolate"

"Honey berry for me please!" said Tayana.

"These are very new to me so I will try cheesy chocolate" said Odeya.

"Good choice!" he said.

"Well I hope this is good! Haven't tried this in years" said Odeya.

"You will enjoy it" she said.

They stood waiting for their snow cream. Odeya needed something to distract her from the recent events that almost claimed her life. It wasn't long when he brought two cups of snow cream, there was layers of chocolate and a icy mist floating on top. Odeya gladly takes it with a smile and they found a shady place to sit. When Odeya took the first bite it was heaven in her mouth, the gooey chocolate melted in her mouth. "oh! this is really good" said Odeya.

"I knew you would like it" said Tayana.

"I used to come here when I was a child but I was always accompanied by Royal Guards even though I wasn't Royalty" said Odeya.

"When will you take me to visit the Palace?" Tayana asked.

"I haven't been home in five years but I will try and arrange a visit" said Odeya.

"Is the food in the Palace different?" Tayana asked.

"I could sneak you in the Royal kitchen if you like and you can tell the royal chefs to make anything you like" said Odeya with a smile.

"Yes! can I take some home?" asked Tayana getting excited.

Odeya smiled at Tayana's excitement.

"I barely eat as I am looking forward to a trip to the Temple of Asteria. It's beautiful at night and you should come with me" Tayana said.

"Yes I heard about it but I won't have the time, I am sorry little one" said Odeya.

"You will love the pathway leading to the Temple, I have seen it in a painting" she said.

"Am sure I will visit soon, I should visit your mother before I return to the Palace" said Odeya.

"I also should return home" said Tayana.

"Will she be working late again? Asked Odeya.

"Yes!"

"Will you be okay?" asked Odeya.

"Yes! I know my way through the market" said Tayana.

"Alright, will see you soon little one" said Odeya as they departed in different directions.

Chapter Four

Odeya, now alone as she entered the busy streets once again, walked down into a narrow walkway to Ayalet's tavern. Belvel was the best known tavern in Arydress and was always filled with people drinking and laughing. Lively music kept the noise level just below a roar. As she walked in she glanced around at the familiar surroundings; taking in the layout including the numerous round wooden tables, the high-backed chairs, the long scarred and stained bar, and a large fireplace with a welcoming fire. A staircase led up to several rooms which were rented to travelers. As she examined the patrons for familiar faces someone shouted. "Odeya! Is that you?"

"What have you done with your hair, you look amazing!" he said.

"Clytius, what are you going here? Where is Ayalet?" asked Odeya.

Clytius was Ayalet's older brother. A good friend to Odeya, always giving her advice. He was more like a brother to her, very protective. Odeya frowned when she looked at a scar on his left cheek. Some years ago before Odeya could go for training, she was attacked by a group of thieves, Clytius saved her but both of them were badly wounded. The thieves got away with the Royal shield of Arydress, the symbol of the Empire.

Avril send her Royal guards to search for it but with no luck. At that time, Clytius, although injured himself, never left her side until she was fully recovered.

"So are you working here?"

"Not really just helping out my little sister" he said.

"Ah yes, the spring festival. It gets really busy this time of the year" said Odeya.

"Can't wait for the feast" said Clytius.

"So you heading for the Royal Palace?" asked Clytius.

"Later! May I have a glass of water." she asked.

"Just water?" he said in surprise.

"We have the best wines in Arydress and you asking for water!" he said.

Odeya smiled as he poured her a glass of water, she missed the company of her friends and drinking wine at the Palace. It's been many years and she has forgotten the taste of all the local wines. She know this tavern was but it wasn't a good time to have wine, she just needed rest and some peace.

"So Odeya! Would you like anything else?" he asked.

"Yes please, I would like to rent a room" she said.

"I will arrange one of the finest room in this tavern, I think my sister was saving this for you, she just stepped out a while ago but she should be back any time now" he said.

"Alright then, I will be waiting for her in my room, oh and would you mind to please send some food up to my room later, I also need a hot bath" said Odeya.

"Sure thing Odeya, your meal will be ready in no time; give me a minute I will find the key" he said.

Odeya handed over hundred Silver Drachmas but he refused to accept money from her. Odeya sipped the water, it was heaven to her. She felt the cool water go down her throat as she gulped the water down. As she placed the glass back on the table, Clytius returned. "I hope you will like the room" he said.

She gladly took the key from him and without a word she made her way to the room. It felt like an effort to climb up the stairs. With each step she took, a small part of her energy was left behind. She made it to the door. She felt she could pass out any minute. The door had some tiny paint flakes peeled off at the bottom. Ayalet hadn't repainted the door but who could blame her, she hardly had the time, the tavern was also busy and there was lots to do to daily preparing for the evening guests.

Odeya quickly took the key to open the door. The room was small, airy and clean. The walls were the colour of the sea, a light sea blue. The wooden floor creaked when she walked across it. A small square table near the bed had only three chairs around it and an empty bowl in the centre. It was somewhat cozy and perfect, she didn't care about the size of the room or the colour, all she cared about was getting some sleep. It was not long when there was a knock at the door. She quickly opened it hoping it was Ayalet but it was a servant holding some fresh towels and three bath robes, one was of pink silk.

"I'm Lenna and I'm here to help prepare a bath for you." she said.

"Yes a bath! I really need it! Thank You." said Odeya.

Odeya gladly let her pass and she quickly got to work, Odeya sat on the bed and watched her pour the clear water into the round wooden tub. She placed a red crystal into the water to bring it to a perfect temperature, she then put five drops of white liquid into the water and it slowly turned into a shiny white colour. "Your bath is ready, let me help you" said Lenna.

Odeya was never shy when it came to revealing herself to others. Lenna gently loosens the belt from the dress. "This is a beautiful design, who made it?" she asked.

"I wouldn't know and it's a long story." said Odeya.

"I will take your dress to be cleaned and will give you some time alone" said Lenna.

Odeya finally alone in the empty room, tested the water, it was a perfect temperature so she stepped into the hot bath. She submerged her entire self in the steamy water. She remained under the water for a minute just to clear her mind, the assassin she encountered troubled her. She tried so hard to remember what had happened and who the mysterious little girl at the Palace of Helios was. So many questions needed to be answered. She surfaced and wiped the water from her face.

"Helios, divine God of the Sun, I call upon you to guide me to the truth. Let your radiant light fill me."

Odeya waited for something to happen but nothing did, the room remained silent. She was fooling herself, Titans don't appear often. Her tummy rumbled from the lack of food, maybe that was the reason why she felt so weak and drained. She wanted to spend more time in the bath but she had to get something to eat before she faints. She used the sponge to rub her body before she stepped out. She heard a knock on the door, "Odeya! It's me Ayalet."

"I'll be there in a second" she grabbed her bath robe before she opened the door. The joy she felt was overwhelming when she opened the door to greet her friend.

"Odeya!" said Ayalet

"Yes it's me" said Odeya.

"Why is your hair black?" asked Ayalet.

"It's good to see you, friend" said Odeya.

"Where is the tray with the food, I'm starving?" asked Odeya.

"It's right here!" said Clytius.

He walked in and placed the tray on the table, "I made your favorite, hope you like it" he said.

"You made Lintro chicken for me? How sweet of you" said Odeya.

"We really missed you." said Ayalet.

They both hugged Odeya, a single tear rolled down her cheek, having friends by her side really made her feel loved. All her fears, her grief, her pain vanished when her friends were near. "Thank You!" said Odeya.

"Hey… no tears, we will always be there for you" said Clytius.

Odeya wiped her tears while Clytius poured the hot spiced tea. "Here drink this, it will help take the stress away" he said.

"Thanks" said Odeya.

The tea was a good combination with Lintro chicken and hot buns soaked in a creamy potato sauce.

"Afraid I have to leave, got some stuff that needs taking care of" he said.

"Wait, you are not staying? I was hoping you would share a meal with me." Said Odeya.

He could see the disappointment in her eyes, he had a good heart and couldn't say no to a dear friend. "I want to hear everything about your training" he said.

All three take a seat and listened to Odeya's story until the very end while she enjoyed her meal that he had prepared for her. "Tell me, what do you know about the Black Rose?" asked Odeya.

"Black Rose? It's just a mythical story told in ancient times. That's all I know" said Ayalet.

"Why are you so interested in this black rose?" asked Clytius.

"I forgot to mention why I was attacked by an assassin" said Odeya changing the topic.

"I stole a box. I think he was guarding the ancient black box and I think it belonged to Helios, I have stolen something from the Gods. When the assassin struck me, I remembered the assassin's blade struck deep into my chest, I was sure to die but something strange happened, I fell into a semi dream like sleep and when I woke there was no sign of the assassin and my wounds had healed."

Clytius became concerned for her when she mentioned the assassin. "I heard rumors that the Royal Palace was attacked by an Assassin but not sure if it's true." said Clytius.

"I am sure it's just rumors Odeya! Don't get too worried." said Ayalet.

"Could it be linked to some kind of darkness?" asked Odeya.

"I wouldn't know anything about that but the Palace defenses are impossible to penetrate and the queen's soldiers are well trained. Oh and by the way the Leader of the elite soldiers is irresistible handsome, love his smile and my God his eyes" said Ayalet with a smile on her face.

Both stare at Ayalet. Odeya knew that she was talking about Atreus and this was his favorite place to eat.

Odeya remembers the time when Ayalet first met him. It was a hot summer day and a group of travelers stopped at the tavern for a drink before they pass through. It was packed with lively people and Ayalet was running low on drinks. Her food and suppliers where delayed so she decided to close the tavern for a few hours but the group refused to leave. They demanded for Ayalet to entertain them and refused to pay for their drinks. Ayalet tried to reason with them but with no luck. Just as Ayalet was starting to get frustrated a tall muscular man entered coming to her rescue. He was huge, his eyes so mysterious and he wore the black Royal outfit. He spoke and the entire tavern become silent, this made the group pay and leave. Ayalet wanted to thank him but no words came out. From that day she was been dreaming about him but when he visits the tavern she was too shy to say hello even if she summoned up the courage she could never approach him.

"Ayalet, my dear friend I know about your feelings for Atreus but I'm afraid he is off-limits. Forgive me if I sound hush." said Odeya.

"I know but wish I could have just one kiss." said Ayalet.

"There is something I could do but Avril cannot find out. It needs to be done in secret. I will speak with Atreus as a friend." said Odeya.

"Please, just to look at his handsome face again, it will give me joy." said Ayalet.

"My sister has truly lost it, anyway I need to go back to work, will see you down later." said Clytius.

"Will meet you down in a second." said Ayalet. Clytius left the room. Odeya stared at the closed door as if the assassin could come busting through the door, she still couldn't get him out of her mind. She looked down at her plate hoping the nightmare will vanish. A smile was on her face to hide the pain from her dearest friend.

~***~

Odeya was finally alone in the room, she needed rest from the nightmare she had encountered. She flopped on the soft bed, the tiredness took a toll on her body. She felt like she could sleep for a week. It wasn't long until her heavy eyes closed and she falls into a deep sleep. Dreams filled her mind, dreams of the stranger in the forest whispering her name. Odeya slept for hours and when she was awoke she realized that it was already night, a warm fire lit up the room. She sat up on the bed and looked around, she felt a presence near her like the feeling that she felt in the forest. There was a warm feeling inside her, like someone from her past life was close.

"Please if you are there, please show yourself?" said Odeya.

She closed her eyes and tried to force on the feeling to linger but it disappeared the moment she heard a knock on the door. She took in a deep breath before opening the door. "Hello again I'm sorry to disturb you but I thought you would like a hot meal before bed" said Lenna.

"I must have slept the entire day" said Odeya. Lenna walked passed Odeya to place the tray on the table, she poured a glass of cold water and handed it over to Odeya. She then left the room, closing the door behind her. Odeya could sense something different about her but she brushed the feeling aside as if it was nothing. Odeya took a seat next to the raging fire, she felt relaxed so decided to read the Lexicon. She summoned her book, flipped to the back of the book and found drawing of some unknown pattern. She touched the drawing and it started to glow. Words appeared:

Forbidden Ancient Gates of Aveileya

All gates lead to the ruined cities of Aveileya.
Crystal Sky
Crystal Sea
Crystal Fire
Crystal Sun
Crystal Chaos
Reopening the Gates that was once sealed by two
powerful Gods after darkness consumed worlds.

The blood of a mortal God is the key to open all gates.
The five gates are:
Shadow Gate
The Sky Gate
Water Gate
Fire Gate
&
The Gates of Chaos

If the gates should open then darkness will consume
other worlds.

Odeya closed the book in horror placed it on the table but it magical opened again. She looked at the page it opened to and she found markings that matched the ones on her hand but she was unable to read it.

りゅう かつりょくかげ やみ あらし

She closed the book again, Odeya decided it was best to study the book in Avril's Library, it will be quiet and peaceful. Odeya touched the cover of the book and it disappeared. She turned to look at the food, a fire stone was placed near the copper pot to keep it warm. She opened it and found venison stew with freshly baked rolls on the side. Odeya though that she was not hungry but the stew was so delicious that she emptied the pot. She then relaxed on the comfy bed listening to the fire and hoped that she could fall off to sleep again, she needed to get as much rest as possible.

~***~

Sunlight brighten the room as Odeya slowly awakened fully recovered and refreshed, all her energy returned. She slowly climbed out of bed, she felt her bare feet sink into something soft and grainy and she felt the heat the moment she stepped on it. She looked down at the floor, the entire floor was covered in hot desert sand. Her dreams and visions could cause her power to be uncontrollable. Drawing wind energy from within and slowly the sand dispersed. She closed her eyes and tried to remember her vision. She used her dream energy to recall her vision. She finds herself in a dark passageway and the torches on the wall provided little light. The floor was covered with hot sand which explained the sand in her room. She was in shock when she noticed that her outfit was full black and a hood was up, her boots were heavy like it was meant for a warrior. She had her bow and quivers strapped across her back. She continued to walk down the dimly lit passage unaware of what awaited her at the end. As she walked, she could feel a slight breeze, the air was coming directly in front of her. The light got brighter. She soon came to a slightly opened door, she bravely opened it and walked in. The colossal chamber had a massive God imprisoned in chains, his muscular body bound in Crystal. Then it occurred that he could be a Titan but who could have imprisoned him and why.

"Odeya!" he shouted.

His voice sounded powerful and shook the entire chamber, her vision ended the moment he opened his eyes.

Odeya could feel his power. He was definitely a Titan but she couldn't make sense of her vision. She decided to write it in her book so she could get a better understanding of it. She spent an hour writing her vision. She slowly closed the book, a relief filled her. She didn't notice before but her dress was ready and it hung on the wall. "Maybe it's time I leave" she whispered to herself. She had been in her bath robe for too long. She quickly slipped it out revealing her nakedness, a cool breeze blew from the opened window. She gentle stepped into the bath and closed her eyes calming her mind. Thoughts of herself lying on the soft grass in the Royal Gardens in Avril's Palace and the sound of the water fountain in the centre flowed gently through her mind. The trees all around provided shade from the burning sun. Odeya spent most of her time in the Gardens in her young days, reading books from the Royal Library.

~***~

Odeya prepares herself before she heads down but noticed that the same gold boots she wear at Helios Palace or Temple was placed next to her dress. "well this is truly the work of God" she whispered.

Ayalet's tavern wasn't so busy in the mornings, only a young man occupied a table at the far corner as if she didn't want to be disturbed.

"Please tell me you have Lintro Chicken" she asked the waitress.

"Yes we do but it will take about 20 mins to prepare so would you like something to drink while you wait? "she asked.

Apple juice would be nice" said Odeya.

"Alright, I will be back shortly" said the waitress.

"Good morning Ayalet, need some help before I leave, I could spare an hour?" asked Odeya.

"Oh yes please! Take this to the young gentlemen seated in the far table to your right "

"Sure!" said Odeya.

As Odeya placed the meal on the table, a young woman came storming into the tavern holding a weapon that looked more like a samurai sword. Her stormy grey eyes revealed a mysterious side within her. Her long black hair reminded her of the shadow warriors. She did looked a little pale but Odeya sensed her boundless energy. The clothes she wore revealed that she was different and definitely not from this land. Similar to Kimono style.

"I am Lafera, I am looking for the Daughter of War. Odeya!" She yelled.

"What's going on?" asked Odeya.

"We need to leave now, the Goddess has found you! Said the young woman.

"What are you talking about? Asked Odeya more shocked then confused.

"Oh no, it's too late! The darkness is alright here" the woman yelled.

Odeya turned towards Ayalet but noticed a sudden darkness that brought a chill into the tavern. A pool of black ice formed on the floor. Three dark shaped abovet the pool released a burning smell as if they were created in the depths of hell.

"Don't move!" said the young women.

As the three dark figures took the shape of beasts. Odeya could see their black ash coat and their blood red eyes scanning the room. Fear consumed her when they let out a howl, revealing their razor sharp teeth that could rip out flesh in seconds. When Odeya stepped back she accidental bumped the table next to her. One of the beast raced towards her. She stood frozen in fear. A mysterious warrior materialized just in front of her to save her from a fatal attack. "Kuso!" he yelled.

"Don't move just remain where you are, I got this" said the mysterious warrior. He quickly removed his katana from its sheath.

Somehow the sound of his voice brought a calmness to her soul but she could not relax, not yet; she was still in a dangerous situation. These beasts were hell hounds. The young warrior glanced at his Katana, the hell hounds also feeds off fear, one of the hell hounds stepped closer to Ayalet. She closed her eyes but dared not scream, it felt her fear.

Lafera distracted them with a shuriken that appeared in her hands. Two more hellhounds bolted towards them while the third one moved passed the warrior with speed and pounced on Odeya from the back, she fell violently to the ground and lost the grip of her dagger, its sharp claws ripped through her dress tearing deep into her flesh. Loud screams escape her lungs. She felt its large jaws that gripped onto her shoulder pinning her down.

She held out her hand, using her power, the dagger moved straight into the beast's eye. To her relief the beast released her from its grip. Odeya managed to crawl away but still she was not out of danger. The warrior could see she was in serious trouble, rushed in to save her.

Ayalet stood frozen against the wall, watching the horror unfold. Who was this mysterious person battling the hounds, he moved with incredible speed, she watched as he took down the hell hounds with just one weapon. Ayalet now free, rushed to Odeya's side, slowly turned her over but still aware of the hounds that were near. To her relief Odeya was still alive but barely holding on. She needed to get Odeya away from the hounds, she hoped for a little help from her brother but he stepped out not knowing when he will return. As the warrior took down the last hell hound, Ayalet dragged Odeya behind the bar table. She noticed Odeya slowly slipping away. "No Odeya! Stay with me!" yelled Ayalet.

Ayalet held onto her hand, Odeya's wounds were so deep it was impossible for her to recover. Lafera came to her aid, and dropped down to her knees. "Quick! Get me a tavozin leaves and alofon paste, I know you have the ingredients stocked" said Lafera.

"There is no need for that, clearly you losing your gift" he said to Lafera. The shadow warrior knelt down beside Odeya, gently lifted her up slightly and placed his one hand on her chest.

"Odeya! Guardian! Listen to my voice! Let my shadow guide you back into the light!" he said.

Ayalet was in shock when Odeya's wounds slowly began to heal. She never witnessed anything like this before. Odeya slowly opened her eyes and glanced up at the warrior. "Jin! Your name is Jin" whispered Odeya.

Odeya held onto him but slipped back into an unconscious state. "Quick! Take her back to her room" said Ayalet.

She guided him up the stairs, forced the door open, almost stumbled when she stepped into the room and the warrior followed close behind. He gentle placed Odeya onto the bed. "Will she be okay?" Ayalet asked.

"Yes! You are brave young warrior." he said.

"where did those hell hounds come from?" asked Ayalet.

Lafera stepped into the room, all thoughts were forced on Odeya. "those were not hell hounds. It is something similar. Hell hounds only spawn if there is death. Its called Anayins used by Assassins or solidiers of Hades. They track and destroy" said Lafera.

"Will we be safe and will Odeya be okay?" asked Ayalet.

"Yes! They wont attack any time soon again, as for Odeya her rune markings will help her heal" she said.

"We should leave, got to stop another bounty" he said.

"Are you hunters?" Ayalet asked.

"I am a Guardian and this is a Shadow created by my brother for my protection but he is no longer with us" said the warrior.

He placed his Kitana sword beside Odeya while Lafera opened up a red mist portal, Ayalet had never seen such powerful magic before. She wished to lean more about them but they left.

"We will meet again" said Lafera.

They both vanished into the misty portal.

Chapter Five

Odeya awakened in an empty room; she quickly climbed out of bed, troubled. She remembered every word he said but there was no sign of him. She found a katana on the floor. The moment she picked up the white katana, she could feel its energy. It felt like a thousand raging storms in the palm of her hands. No mortal could craft a powerful weapon such as this. There was Japanese markings on the blade. She placed it back into its sheath when she heard the door creek open.

She was so glad to see it was Clytius, "Odeya! I heard what happened! You still okay?" he asked.

"Barely!" said Odeya.

"The place is a mess never seen anything like this before!" said Clytius.

"How is Ayalet? Is she alright?" asked Odeya.

Clytius nodded.

"It was so horrible, I don't understand why is this happening, I need to find answers. This mess started when I stole something from the Gods" said Odeya.

He stood there not sure what to make of everything. "anyway I got to get back and help my sister, the place looks like hell" he said.

"I will be down in a second just need some time to think" Odeya said.

"are you sure you okay?" asked Clytius once again out of concern.

"Yes!" said Odeya.

She stood silent as she watched him shut the door, she wondered if she visited the Palace if she would put Avril in danger. She hadn't seen her for years. She glanced at the Katana once again she held in her hand hoping to get a vision, but nothing happened. She strapped it around her back and prepared to leave.

~ *** ~

Odeya walked slowly down the stairs and across the broken bottles and ash towards Ayalet. "Odeya! I'm so glad you are okay! Not sure about healing magic he had used but he saved your life" said Ayalet.

"I had a vision of him but it wasn't clear, his name is Jin! That's all I know" said Odeya.

"Never heard of him but the young lady said you will be safe for now and you will meet again" said Ayalet.

"Forgive me but I must leave! I need to find information about the Black Rose and if its linked to any of the attacks I just encountered" said Odeya.

"Will you return? Clytius asked.

"Yes I am sure I will, I also promised Tayana a visit to the Palace" said Odeya.

"Tayana! I need to check on her. Goodbye Odeya we will meet again" said Ayalet.

She hugged Odeya gently knowing that she wasn't fully recovered from her nightmare. With her bag safely across her back and the Katana, Odeya makes her way out. As Odeya stepped out into the street, without any warning a vision surfaced. She found herself standing next to a frozen lake. She could see a little girl approaching bringing with her an icy wind. She had beautiful green eyes with silver-white hair which fell over her shoulders. Odeya was shocked to find that she was the same little girl she encountered at the Palace of Helios.

The child touched Odeya's face. Odeya could see a tear rolling down her cheek, a sad expression on the little girl's face but when Odeya wiped the tear the girl disappeared like dust blowing in the wind. The environment changed she heard a war horn in the distance. She noticed the black clouds darkening the sky from the north, which trembled with a breaking raging storm. It drenched the ground. Odeya's boots sank into the waterlogged ground. She looked behind her and saw an army of soldiers. These were no ordinary soldiers. She could not see their faces as every soldier had a mask and held two katana swords. They also had very little armor and no shields at all. She felt a powerful energy within them as if they were built for one purpose only and that was to fight. It was the same energy she felt when she came into contact with the hooded warrior, but something was a different about these soldiers. A young woman appeared in front of the army. It appeared as if she was leading the army. Before Odeya could study this mysterious woman, her vison ended. Before she tried to make sense of it a male voice behind startled her. The unknown strange smiled as she turned to face him.

"Who are you?" she asked.

"Ichiro! Avril's personal chef but don't think we have met before, although I have been working in the Palace for many years" he said.

"Now we finally meet, how strange is that" said Odeya.

"Are you heading to the Palace, may I accompany you after I am done?" he asked.

"Yes I gladly accept!" said Odeya.

"So why are you away from the Palace?" Odeya asked.

"I was asked to bring in some rare ingredients from the Hydran market." he said.

"You been to the market, what is it like? Will you take me there someday?" Odeya asked.

"Trust me! its not safe, if you haven't been there you will easily get yourself lost or worse, killed!" he said.

"I think I can handle myself!" said Odeya.

"Anyway, why are we having this conversation in the middle of the street?" asked Odeya.

"I will meet you back here when I'm ready!" he said.

~***~

Ichiro watched her disappear into the busy streets, he needed her to leave before he could set his plan in motion. He quickly made his way to a corner of narrow streets. There was no poverty in Arydress and the streets were also kept clean. Arydress was the largest city in Eradonis and the Empire fought to keep it the way it was.

He came to a large red door with the name Sneaky Dragon above the door. He pushed the heavy doors open. It was empty which; was a relief. Sneaky Dragon was the second largest tavern in Arydress. "Hello! Is anyone here?"

Long seconds pass when a familiar voice greet him. "Ichiro in disguise! You even fooled me!"

"Ryu! What are you doing in Eradonis?" asked Ichiro.

"Well the Prince asked for help so I'm here. All the wooded creates are already in the Palace waiting to be opened so you better hurry" said Ryu.

"I guess I owe you" said Ichiro.

"So are you still after the Zail's fire nymph? If he found out what you doing, he will skin you alive!" said Ichiro.

"That won't happen. You better get going." said Ryu.

"The darkness is growing not even Delos will be safe when it dark. Be safe friend" said Ichiro.

Ryu's calmness about the situation proved that he was strong. Ichiro had been a good friend for years but there was a dark secret about him.

~***~

Ichiro slowly made his way back, Odeya was already there waiting. "Lets get going before the Empress throws a fit, she gets really grumpy when her food is not on time!" said Ichiro.

He chuckled as they both take a slow stroll to the Palace. "So tell me are you sure we haven't met before?" She asked.

"Well the Palace is a huge place and I prefer to work alone" he said.

"Do you have any family or friends?" she asked trying to make conversation.

"Yes but that's a sad story" said Ichiro.

"Tell me." she said.

"You sure you want to know?" he asked.

"Yes!" said Odeya.

"I was born in an unhappy family, my mother hated me and as for my father he was always commanding me, training me and the worst of all he used to use torture when I didn't obey" said Ichiro.

"That's awful" she said.

"There was no love, I was a pawn to them. The only person that they cared for was my sister, well half sister. She was also under my fathers command, always obeying; never to question him"

"So I'm guessing you escaped him with your sister, am I right?" Odeya asked.

"Yes but it wasn't a happy ending, my sister was captured and ravaged by an evil man." said Ichiro.

 A long silence filled the air as they reach the Palace gates, Odeya was shaken by his words. She didn't know how to comfort him, he looked strong and it seemed like nothing could break him.

~***~

The Royal Palace was built by the Ancients and made with solid red and white marble, it was impossible to penetrate the palace walls and it could withstand any attack. The palace was stretched across on a large Cliffside. There was a massive bridge leading to the fortress with pillars all lined in a row. The design of the pillars and wide arches made it unique. This brings out the beauty of the Palace. The guards that blocked the entrance recognized Odeya, greeted her and let her in.

They both walked towards the opened gate that led into the garden entrance. Rows of beautiful red flowers filled the place making it looked like the gardens of
Eden.

"Well I'm afraid this is where we part ways." said Ichiro.
"I would like to spend more time and get to know you better, if it's okay with you?" Odeya asked.

"Afraid that won't happen" said Ichiro.

"Why?" Odeya asked.

"I shall be returning home soon, things are going to get worse there, but maybe I will say a quick goodbye before I leave." said Ichiro.

Odeya watched him walk away and realized that there was something that was not right about him. Why was he so mysterious, she could tell he was hiding something.

~***~

As soon as Odeya entered the massive Throne room, all the soldiers turned to face her as if they were expecting her; or were they waiting for someone else to walk in through the door. Frozen in place, she hadn't been to the Palace in five years and something was clearly not right.

Everyone in Arydress knew that the Royal army was not to be trifled with, they were strong and fierce and trained at a young age. Some soldiers even fight in the Arena to prove their strength. Avril kept her soldiers in check and if they disobeyed they were brutally punished.

The soldiers step aside as she nervously makes her way towards Avril. She climbed the staircase which was made out of fire gems that gave it a unique style. Behind the Throne there was seven black doors which Odeya was forbidden to enter.

What secrets were hidden deep inside the Palace? The seven black rooms remained sealed not even the Empress knew what was down there.

The Throne in front of her had a design of a sleeping dragon. The ancients that build the Palace knew what they were doing. The sky roof was breathtaking, the floor had a black and red pattern which made the room look beautiful.

Two soldiers held a prisoner, his chains were tightly bound around his wrists. Although he had a scar on his face he was attractive. She then noticed that the Royal advisors were present which meant trouble.

"Odeya! Sister I'm so glad to see you" said Avril.
"It's been years!" said Odeya smiling.

Avril hugged her tight but their reunion was cut short by the advisors.
"Take him back to his prison! I will deal with him later" said Avril.

"I heard about the assassin, is it true?" Odeya asked.

The soldiers removed him from the Throne room. The advisors then requested that Odeya leaves as she does not belong there. She disliked the advisors and it was also offensive to Odeya for she was not Royalty.

"I guess I'm not welcomed here" said Odeya.

"We will talk about this later. How about we meet at the gardens when I am done with this prisoner and I will send some hand-maidens to pamper you, you look a mess" said Avril.

"That would be lovely" said Odeya.

The guards escorted Odeya to her Royal bedroom. She could finally relax for a bit before she heads for the library. Odeya's room was huge and airy. The guards closed the doors behind her. She crossed the room passed the large mahogany furniture on her way towards her bed. She needed to hide the katana sword and the black ancient box to keep it safe from enemy eyes. It was thanks to her training she knew how to hide stuff from others.

She stood near the mirror and placed the tips of her fingers on the mirror, focusing on the spell she was about to say.

Escondido en segredo
Déixao estar
Non visto
En Shadow's Light

Hidden in Secret
Let it be
Unseen
In Shadow's Light

The sword and the box shimmered into a silver liquid and vanished. Odeya was so glad to be back in her room and the soft bed brought a smile to her face. She flopped onto the bed, rolled around on the silk sheets and loved the softness against her skin. It brought joy and comfort to her, she was home.

She got up and removed her boots, she walked across the cool floor out into the balcony. She sat on a comfy chair and closed her eyes enjoying the cool breeze; forgetting the nightmare of the past few days.

She didn't care about her early encounters with the stranger or the hellhounds. She listened to the sound of the wind flowing through the trees. A calmness filled her mind but she dared not sleep as she took in the fresh air. Every moment was precious to her and she missed being treated like a princess. It was not long before her hand-maidens enter. They were all excited to welcome Odeya back. Immediately they took her to the Royal baths.

They walk across a stone pathway into a large building. The doors were also made of solid black wood. The guards opened it and Odeya stepped inside. It was breath-taking. The glass roof above was designed with crystals hanging down. It dissolved the air and turned it into a crystal oil which dropped onto a marble stone table. The oil was used to make the skin glow. Several pools with both hot and cold water were filled with a shiny red and silver pearls. Some pools displayed a shiny silver liquid, which is an ancient oil harvested from the Tavozin flowers. It is used to soften the skin and heal injuries. Odeya walked across the shimmering cool red floor and scanned the paintings on the wall, paintings of past Empresses that ruled before Avril. Pillars were all lined in a row and statues of water maidens pouring water as fountains into the pools. The hand-maidens remove her clothes and tied her hair using clips. They take her into a circled ring bath and her feet touched a cool liquid.

They use a leaf shaped bowl to gently pour warm water onto her body. She closed her eyes and all her pain, fears and anger began to wash away. They gently rubbed a silky white soap on her entire body. She loved being pampered and wanted it to last. They then use a gel to cover her body and took her to another circle rind. Steam melted the gel slowly until it came off completely. Then Odeya stepped into the third pool and soaked up the oil. She relaxed her body enjoying the hot oil. She enjoyed long minutes of pure relaxation before she stepped out of the pool. The maidens dried her with a towel and she then lays on the stone table. The droplets of red oil fall onto her body and they gently rubbed it onto her entire body. While she lays on the table they unclipped her beautiful long hair pouring water over it. They used a sweet smelling liquid on her hair. Hot and cool air blows onto her body, she enjoyed the ten minutes of pure bliss. Then the hand-maidens wash away the liquid on her hair gently lifted her up and poured water again over her body to wash away the oil. They put on a red bath robe to cover her naked body. She took her finger tips and magically dried her hair and the maidens gasp in amazement. She relaxed on the soft pillows and they offered her chocolates, she gladly took the whole tray. Then they leave her to relax for a bit. She listened to the sound of the water fountains, the sounds were so soothing and she could fall asleep at any moment. She didn't want this to end she could lie in the pool for hours. Soon the hand maidens return and removed her bath rope, they rub a cool cream on her body and they dress her in new clothes. It was a design that Odeya loved, something similar to the Lexicon black Kimono outfit. They set her hair in an up-style but leaves strands of it hanging down. Odeya helped herself to more chocolate, eating every last one. She decided to delay her visit to the library, she could use some rest.

~***~

The few hours alone in her room was total tranquility and she felt it was time to visit the Grand Library.

She knew her way and entered the Grand Library. It was a huge dome like building with connected gardens and it was filled with ancient scrolls and books. There were three levels with swirling staircases leading to the upper flours. It also had many reading rooms. Rows of books stacked ceiling high in the shelves and maps that stretched across the walls, filled the library. She walked to the section where the ancient scrolls were kept. There was so many it could take days to go through all of them. The scrolls were so old that they were not catalogued. She grabbed as many as she could carry and placed them on the table, she went back for more until the table becomes full. She took a seat and got to work. She broke the seal of the first scroll she found. The writings were written in black ash, she reads it but finds no information. Every scroll she opened was interesting but nothing led to the black rose or the strange temple she found, not a single clue. Odeya went back to the shelves and she found a mysterious black scroll hidden beneath some other scrolls. She quickly grabbed it.

"Another black scroll!" She broke the seal revealing an ancient language and the rest of the words were faded, Odeya could not make sense of it. She decided to take the scroll with her hoping to unlock its secrets. Odeya was tired of searching and felt that she was wasting time trying to find something that is a myth. She looked around, the library was a mess, opened scrolls lying all over the floor.

When Odeya looked up she found Avril approaching her carrying Astarlin.

"Astarlin has been causing a lot of trouble in the Palace, better take care of your pet." said Avril.
"I am so glad he is safe" said Odeya.

She grabbed him, held him close but when she placed him down he goes off running towards the door. Odeya was confused; was it her magic that scared him.

"That's very strange!" said Odeya.
"We will find him, but tell me about yourself; I would like to know where have you been all these years and why has your hair turn black? What is going on Odeya?" Avril asked.
"Long story! I was dragged away and forced into training, something about Guardians." said Odeya.

"It has been five years, I even sent my Royal Guards to look for you. I even lost hope, thought you were dead." said Avril.

"I survived it but while I was in training a heard that Haniel was missing so when my training ended I went straight to the Temple to look for her but the Temple has been destroyed and there was no sign of the priestess" said Odeya.

"You think she is still alive?" Avril asked.

"Am not sure, there was no indication of her death so let us hope." said Odeya.

"Well I need to leave now we will meet at the gardens soon, I need to prevent a war and with the feast in a few days, it will make it difficult"

"War? What have I missed?" Odeya asked.

"The Prince of Siacodia has been killed, he was the one I was meant to marry, alliance has been broken so I need to find another solution or this will lead to war." said Avril.

"That does not sound good! Was that the reason for the assassination attempt?" asked Odeya.

"No! Something was different about the assassin, he was stronger and faster, I barely escaped." said Avril.

"I think I can help, do you want to see what I have learnt in my years of training?" Odeya asked.

"Alright, I could spare ten minutes" said Avril.

Avril takes a seat as the room began to freeze. Snow began to fall inside the library and soon the floor was covered in thick snow. Odeya then used the power of fire. She heats up the room and the snow started to melt and water flooded the library floor, Avril stood up in shock. The heat dried the water and formed storm clouds and the room became dark and eerie as raindrops fall, lightning flashed. Avril was drenched, the icy wind made her shiver. She waved her hand and the clouds disappear and the room turned back to normal. Avril was more surprised that the books and the scrolls were not affect by the water and snow. Odeya used the tip of her finger and slowly ran her finger down her hand to draw the water out. Avril was dry once again. Odeya wanted to show her more but that was for another time. There was so many things she wanted to share with Avril but did not know where to begin.

"Elements of the best part of the training" said Odeya.

"This is truly amazing! I shall delay my royal meeting, come let's take a walk to the gardens, I could use a small break from royal duties" said Avril.

"That would be great!" said Odeya.

They both walked towards the gardens and kept the conservation light. The gardens were beautiful, the different rows of flowers filled the entire garden, stone benches were all around and the fountains were huge. Avril stretched herself on the soft grass, taking in nature. She missed the company of Odeya and she was glad to have her back. Avril was taking strain as a Royal and longed for freedom, just for a little time anyway, away from her royal duties.

"Tell me about Ichiro"

"What do you want to know?" Avril asked.

"How long has he been your personal chef?" Odeya asked.

"Ten years if I'm correct. Atreus found him badly wounded and there was some strange markings on him including a sun tattoo on his left shoulder. Said Avril.

"Wait? A sun tattoo? Was it silver or gold?" asked Odeya.

"I'm afraid I don't remember" said Avril.

"He also had the symbol of Arydress on his back so Atreus brought him to the Palace." said Avril.

"Okay that's something I was not expecting. He has a sun tattoo, I need to see it. Tell me where would I find his sleeping quarters?" Odeya asked.

"Odeya! What has gotten you so curious about Ichiro?" Avril asked.

"I just feel like I know him." said Odeya.

Two guards approach them reminding the Empress
that she is needed back at the meeting hall. She had to
leave to attend to her Royal duties; Odeya watched as
she walked away, she felt alone again. Avril and Odeya
could not spend much time together; Royal duties
took most of Avril's time. Odeya sat in silence enjoying
the fresh air. She took a slow walk in the gardens
trying to clear her mind.

Chapter 6

The next morning Odeya felt a lot better knowing she was in the Palace. She started her day searching for Ichiro's room, she was afraid but she needed to know his secrets. After two long hours of searching and by using her gifts Odeya finally found his room. She placed her hand onto the door to sense if he was there or not.

She glanced around hoping that no one will see her enter his room. Seeing that she was safe, she slowly turned the handle and walked in. The moment she walked into his room, something about it was familiar it was like a distant memory that surfaced. A warm feeling passed through her.

She didn't let that distract her. She needed to find information about Ichiro and leave before he returns.

The curtains were closed and that only allowed a little light to seep into the room. She slowly closed the door and began to search for anything that looked suspicious. In the far corner of the room she could see papers stacked on a table. Cautiously walked towards the table, they were all rare maps of Temples; ones that she hadn't discovered in her research.

Underneath all those maps was some writing but it wasn't in any ancient writings or Greek.

Asteria * Eos * Metis * Pallas * Selene * Prometheus * Rhea * Ophion * Lelantas * Astraeus * Atlas * Clymene * Themis * Mnemosyne * Perses * Styx * Coeus * Dione * Eurynome * Oceanus * Tethys * Crius * Iapetus * Hyperion * Cronus * Thea * Phoebe * Menoetius * Eurybia * Helios * Epimetheus

"These are maps of the Temples of Titans but why is he so interested in the Titans?" she whispered.

She grabbed the map of the Temple Helios. And placed it into her pocket bag hoping then Ichiro will not realize that it was missing. Before Odeya could explore any further she felt the tip of a blade on her back.

"What are you doing in my room? Leave now!" Ichiro yelled.

"Forgive me!" Odeya pleaded.

"You are invading my personal space now get out." Ichiro yelled.

"Do I look like I care?" said Odeya. "and why are you so interest in the Titans?" Odeya asked.

"You think I will show you any mercy?" yelled Ichiro.

"I know you hiding something and I will find out what it is!" said Odeya.

"Leave now!" he yelled.

He lowered his dagger, Odeya turned to face him but silence filled the room. She slowly look her way out but when the door slammed she felt rage. This wasn't a good sign for her.

~***~

Odeya entered her room, she rested her back on the door knowing that royal guards will come busting in at any moment. "Why am I doing this" Odeya whispered. Odeya fighting the tears, she lost all trust in herself the moment she stepped out of Ichiro's room. She needed to be more careful next time. When Odeya looked up, she noticed an arrow stuck in her pillow and a note attached on it. She tried not to let her fear take over again. A feeling like death had entered her room. She pulled the note from the arrow and opened it.

All Three Royal Blood Lines Will Be Wiped Out

&

Darkness will consume all in its part

"Don't touch that arrow!"

"Atreus!" said Odeya. She didn't hear him enter. He took out a silver cloth and wrapped it around the arrow, he carefully pulled it out. "What's going on? Has Ichiro spoken to you?" Odeya asked.

"Ichiro? No!" said Atreus.

"I don't have time to explain, I need to take this to the Siacodian Temple. If I am correct this arrow once belonged to an original Guardian but was stolen by Hades" said Atreus.

"Guardian! I heard that word more than once lately" said Odeya.

"Listen! I have to go but you will be safe here" said Atreus.

"Things at the Palace has gotten worse, there is some dark magic around that is linked to the assassins that attacked the Empress. This needs to end now" said Atreus.

"Wait! Is Avril safe? Was the arrow meant for me or Avril?" Odeya asked.

"Everything will be okay, just trust me! I will find out the truth" said Atreus.

Atreus was always calm in dangerous situations, Odeya has watched him fight in the Arena and his fighting skills were brilliant. It reminded her of the assassin she fought.

"There will be guards at your door so if anything happens, just scream" said Atreus.
"Be safe!" said Odeya.

She know that guards were right outside her door, one scream and they will come to her rescue. She glanced around the empty room, a feeling of being watched brought back all her fears. Odeya curled up on the bed, she didn't even bother to remove her boots. She closed her eyes. With all the confusion she managed to slowly drift off to sleep.

~***~

The loud shattering of glass awakened Odeya from a restless sleep, she sat up on the bed and looked around the dark room. A window had blown open from the strong winds. Lightning flashed which brightened the room for a second then it darkened again. She swiftly got to her feet and went to the opened window, trying not to step on the broken glass. Odeya looked out the window, she could see the raging storm. The air was icy cold, at the same time the another windows blew open, the rain gushed through the opened windows. It was then that she realized that the guards should have entered her chambers when the glass shattered. The noise would have definitely alerted them. She rushed towards the doors opened it and stepped out. She gasped in shock. The guards were lying on the floor in a pool of blood. "Oh no! Avril!" yelled Odeya.

She raced to the Throne room and found the assassin holding a dagger at Avril's throat. "Don't come any closer or she dies" he said.

Odeya held up her right hand facing her palm outwards to summon fire energy but nothing happened. "What happened to… " started Odeya.

"Your magic? Let me see, you are in my presence so your magic is suppressed" said the assassin.

"How is that possible?" asked Odeya.

Odeya didn't know that another assassin had approached her from behind. He gripped onto her, his hands held tightly around her, she could barely move within his grasp. "I want to taste your blood, the blood of a Guardian!" he whispered to Odeya. Before she realized what is happening, she felt a sharp pain on her neck, as he drew blood and took in her power. Her blood dripped from her neck, she could feel a darkness in her that surfaced. His cold hand slid down the top of her dress and cupped her breast. "why you doing this? please stop!" said Odeya.

The assassin suddenly seemed stronger. "Let's play a game shall we? If you can guess my true identity then I will reward you with a kiss and if you fail then my hell hounds will enjoy ripping your beautiful body apart" he said. Avril stood in shock when she saw the massive hell hound materialize in a black liquid, she could not move an inch as the other assassin still had the dagger to her throat. "Hmmm, two strong woman, I like that, so let's begin shall we?"

"Now! Who am I?" he asked.

There was a long pause when Odeya finally broke the silence. "Hades!" she yelled.

"Ah! You smart, little one" he said.

Before she could react he whipped her around and slid his tongue into her mouth. She could taste her own blood as he kissed her, a flash of a memory of the underworld passed through her mind but it was only a glimpse. She could not stop him, he was in control.

He ended the kiss with a smirk across his face. She could tell he enjoyed every minute of it. She looked up towards his face, his eyes were like blackish lava. His cold eyes staring back at her, he was huge. She could see the blood on his lips...

"Now for my next questions" said Hades.
"What do you call the black dust that flows deep in the underworld?"

"Why are you doing this?" asked Odeya.
"Answer the question." said Hades.

Odeya could not find the answer, she turned to face the hell hound, Hades seem to enjoy every minute of it. "Please stop this!" said Odeya.
"I don't know the answer to your stupid question!" Odeya yelled.

The hell hound pounced on her, she fall violently to the ground but Hades waved his hand in the air in time to stop the creature from ripping her apart. It did not move, it just pinned her down.

"I have another idea, one that you will surely enjoy" said Hades. The hell hound then walked back to Hades. She slowly rose from the floor and faced him.
"Let's see if you can fight the temptation." said Hades. A ring of black dust formed around Odeya opening up a portal. She started to panic when her feet slowly

sank into the black liquid. The assassin that was holding Avril lets go and she goes to Odeya's rescue, she tried to pull Odeya out of the pool of black liquid but it consumed them both.

"My plan is working" said Hades.

Chapter 7

She felt lightheaded as the black liquid dissolved into the sand. She could feel cold liquid rush up onto her body. Her hands sank into the sand and forced herself up. Odeya glanced at the sea trying to recognize her surroundings. The moonlight was enchanting, the tiny gold pebbles that lay in the sand glowed brightly like orbs. She picked up a pebble, it glowed brighter in her hand and she wondered what it was made of. The huge waves that crashed onto the shore almost looked silver. Then the memories of Hades came flooding in, she glanced around in search for Avril but she was alone on the sandy shore. "Avril!" she yelled. The only sound that came was from the crashing waves. She dusted the sand out from her hair and looked around again for her friend. Her boots sank into the soft sand as she made her way to a forest that was in front of her.

She could sense powerful magic nearby and with each step she took, the ground glowed from her footsteps. The trees she passed had beautiful red leaves and tiny magic orbs which helped her to see in the dark, they looked more like glowworms, they floated around the trees. Clumps of flowers and thick grass covered the ground. She looked up a the stary night sky. She could hear the leaves rustling from the rush of wind, she felt a warm energy that flowed through her body but she realized that this could not be Eradonis, something was different. It was some other mysterious world; but everything around her was so familiar like a lost memory or something from the past.

She gently touched the bark of a tree and hoping to get a vision, but nothing happened. She couldn't get the thoughts of Hades out from her mind, "why have you brought me here? What is your purpose Hades? Can you hear me?" yelled Odeya. The frustration was building up in her mind. She had no magic, no weapons and was totally lost. Further, without her magic she could not track Avril. She had no clue where Avril was and there was no one in sight to help. Venturing alone in the forest, she came across a blue stone pathway. Upon reaching the end of the path, there stood a silver gate which had the sun engraved in the middle and a moon on either side of the gate. As she stepped closer the gate opened and she bravely walked in.

A cloaked figure stood near a small pool of silver liquid, he turned his head slightly when he sensed her presence. His black cloak had a sliver dragon design on the back of it. "Hades?" she asked. Odeya kept her distance as she could not tell if he was friend or foe so she slowly backed away.

She tripped on a rock but before she could fall the cloaked figure caught her, he moved with incredible speed and she started to feel light-headed then sleepy as if it was all a dream.

~ ***** ~

The mysterious figure carried her to the crystal pool and placed her in it, allowing her body to float. He took out his dagger and cut his palm, with his blood he draw his rune markings on the outer stone of the pool. Although she looked beautiful under the moonlight his intentions was not evil. He brushed her lips with his blood and said words in a different language:

I, Haruto! Call upon the royal line of Guardians
To seal this spell of Lust and desire.
Let her Godly beauty shine upon the one that seeks her desire.
Unbreakable lust and power surface within her to restore the royal line.

Here my words Guardians!

He let three drops of his blood drip into her mouth to seal the spell. "Afypnizo"

He leaned in closer to her ear. "Forgive me!" he whispered.

She remind motionless as he caressed her soft cheek then vanished into a shadow mist.

~*~**

Awakened by the morning sun, she rolled over onto her back.

"Finally! The dead awaken!" said Avril in an angry tone.

She turned to glance at Avril, she rested her back against a tree, Odeya sat up still bewildered at her surroundings and stared at Avril with weary eyes.

"Avril! How did you find me and was there another person with me? Something does not feel right, I am not sure if I had a vision or was it a dream?" asked Odeya.

"You were alone when I found you, I searched for you and there you were! So where do you suppose we are?" Avril asked.

"I have no clue why Hades has brought us here. This place is creepy and I would like to leave this place." she Odeya.

"There was something that Hades mentioned, something to do with my past life, I had a brief glimpse of the underworld when all this started unfolding" said Odeya.

"That's very creepy but now I know who sent the assassins, I must return!" said Avril.

"Hades must be watching our every move" said Odeya.

"Well let's find a way out of this mess" said Avril.

They explored the mystic forest for signs or some way to return home, this world was completely different from Eradonis and she wasn't sure if this world was hostile.

"I wonder how big is this place? We need to keep searching for a village or someone that might help us" said Avril. "I'm sure we'll find something we just have to keep searching" said Odeya.

"I'm just eager to get home" said Avril.

As they continued their search a mystic person materialized in a ray of golden light in front of them, she looked like she was ready for war, and she wore a beautiful gold dress armor. She looked like a Goddess. Was she; Odeya wondered.

"Odeya! Please! Don't be afraid! I meant you no harm. I am the Goddess Athena and I have came to warm you of the dangers that are around you" The mysterious lady said.

"Athena!" said Odeya.

She stood tall, not like mortals, Odeya could feel her divine presence but felt like it wasn't as strong like when she was in the presence of Hades. Why had the Goddess taken a mortal form? she wanted to ask Athena a million questions but felt like it wasn't the best time and place.

"What is this threat you come to warn us about?" asked Odeya.

"I have seen into your future and it does not look good. Everyone that you love will die, killed by Erebus. The Lord of Darkness is truly your darkest enemy" said Athena.

The sound of his name brought a coldness that surfaced within Odeya and it was a thousand times worse then Hades. "I will tell you but I will keep this short." said Athena.

"I managed to intervene in Hades plan and pulled you out before you were taken to the underworld. You are in a world called Delos, created by the Gods." said Athena.

"Delos?" I thought this place was a myth" said Odeya.

"If this place was a myth then you wouldn't be standing here!" said Athena.

"Zeus and I were in the mortal realm when the darkness was released, there was no warning. I made it out of there but Zeus wasn't so lucky. Although I made it safely back to Olympus, the darkness somehow effected my divine essences. It has weakened me" continued Athena.

"Zeus is still trapped in the darkness?" Odeya asked.

"Yes! The darkness is powerful not even the Olympians can withstand the power of Erebus." said Athena.

"We need Zeus back. That is why I have now gifted you with the power of visions to help you on your journey but each vision you have weakens me, this is my choice. Apollo is doing his best to keep me alive so Odeya! My sister please! You are our only hope to bring Zeus home to Olympus" said Athena.

"How would I accomplish such a task on my own?" asked Odeya.

"You will learn more as you journey, I have faith in you!" said Athena.

"What does Hades want from me?" asked Odeya.

"I have limited time I am sorry Odeya but I will tell you more if we meet again" said Athena.

"Please wait, how do I get my magic back from Hades?" Odeya asked.

"Are you strong enough to face Hades? I'm afraid I cannot help you, he too powerful but I know you will figure out a way. I must leave now but we will meet again."

 "Be strong my little sister!" said Athena.

The Goddess vanished in a ray of golden light. Odeya wished she had more time with the Goddess Athena.

"Are you sure that was Athena and not another one of Hades' tricks?" asked Avril.

"I am never sure but according to my research about Greek Gods, Athena is Loyal and one of Zeus's favorites, she will never side with Hades" said Odeya.

"I hope you are right!" said Avril.

~***~

"We should keep moving" said Odeya.

"Are you sure you are okay? You look as if you could rip somebody's head out!" said Avril.

"You don't need to worry about me Avril, I will be fine!" said Odeya.

Athena's words lingered in her head but she dared not stop. They travelled farther north for any signs of civilization. The forest was similar to the Aradeya forest but this was thousand times more captivating. Although the women were fascinated by their surrounding, they grew wary to the unfamiliar world which they knew very little of. Athena hadn't explained much about Delos.

The forest seemed to be endless, the thick trees blocked out the sun and they were not familiar with the glowing fruit. They dared not eat them. They figured it could be some old folk's tale but there is a warning about eating unknown fruit. The wind was strong but wasn't cold like the wind in Eradonis. Every tree that they came across had the same blood red leaves.

Not a word was spoken as they emerged out of the forest into a large open field. Gigantic rocks took up most of the space. "What's this? Some-kind of black sand? Is it volcanic?" asked Avril.

Odeya picked up the black sand and slowly dropped it. She sensed mystic power hidden within the sand. "Let's turn back, I have a bad feeling about this" said Odeya.

They both turn heading back into the forest but they were blocked by an energy shield that separated the forest from the large open field.

"I knew something was not right about this place!" said Odeya.

"Can you break through the shield?" Avril asked.

"I'm afraid not! I have been thinking I don't think Hades took away my magic. I have the feeling he did something or altered my magic so I cannot summon it" said Odeya.

"You will figure it out, you are brilliant with magic" said Avril.

Odeya's touched the shiny black rock hoping to get a vision but Athena's words haunted her once again, every vision she gets weakens the Goddess and she didn't want that to happen. Odeya held onto the rock but still no visions.

The women continued to search for a way out, Odeya's heavy boots sank into the soft sand and she could feel the heat radiating from it. There was no lava or steam rising, which was good. It would have been dangerious but that didn't stop the women from exploring further into the open field.

Something caught Odeya attention, a red crystal orb sticking out from the sand.

"Have you seen anything like this before? It looks like the one from Helios's Palace" said Odeya.

"Your curiosity will get us killed!" said Avril.

"Why do I have the feeling this is linked to Helios." said Odeya.

The red orb began to melt into her hand, the red liquid dripped onto the sand and slowly took the shape of a large red crystal tree. Odeya recognized the shape of an olive tree which was a symbol of Athena. Large white pillars formed from the liquid, black vines crept around the white pillars. A raised platform was created with a few stairs leading to the olive tree.

"Well I certainly wasn't expecting that." said Odeya.

"This is truly a strange world." said Avril.

"What are you doing on the training ground?" asked a voice away from them.

Both woman turn towards the strange men who spoke. Judging by their appearance they looked like warriors. They looked calm and Odeya felt that she could trust these warriors.

Odeya smiled at the warriors as she stepped forward towards them. "Forgive us. I am Odeya! It was the Goddess Athena that brough us to this world but we are lost and hoping to find our way home and this is my childhood friend Avril, Empress of Arydress. It is nice to meet you young warriors" said Odeya.

They stood silent for a moment. "It is an honour to meet such a beautiful young Empress. I am Ryu! Son of Nishikido and this, my sweet Empress is Troy! Prince of Arydress" he said.

The news astonished the woman. Avril wasn't sure what to believe, she struggled to keep her Throne. "another adversary! When will this end?" Avril asked.

"Enough of this! After we done there, we will take you to King of Argos." said Troy.

"Right! Let's get started!" said Ryu.

"Would you mind telling me what's going on?" asked Avril.

"I am Summoning a Fire Guardian" said Ryu.

As Ryu made a circle around them with his blade, he said some words for a spell:

Blood of a Guardian

I summon thee

Let your radiant light shine

On the darkest sea

The circle formed a dark blue flame and beautiful child materialized in the circle of fire. Her wings were blood red which matched the colour of her hair. The short dress she wore was deep orange and she had no shoes which revealed a sun tattoo on her left ankle. Her eyes were like a golden sun which gave her an unusual beauty like one of a Goddess hidden in a mortal form.

Odeya frozen when she saw the sun tattoo, It was another mystery waiting to be solved but at the right time. Very curiously Odeya watched the two strange warriors.

"Harmonia! It's good to see you" said Ryu.

"Ryu! Troy! I am glad you summoned me! Delos will suffer the same fate as in the human world, Erebus is growing stronger each passing day. You won't be able to stop the darkness but you can slow it before Delos is completely covered in darkness" said Harmonia.

"That doesn't sound good! Why are the Gods not helping? Surely Apollo will defend this world. It was build by the Gods" said Troy.

"Gods? They are losing this battle but only the chosen few will end the darkness. A journey will start at the Dragon Temple" said Harmonia.

"Well! How much time do we have?" Ryu asked.

Something startled Harmonia, the air around them began to thin and it was becoming hard to breath. Crystal dust filled in the air which made it difficult to see. Ryu started to get close to Harmonia, to protect her from the unknown threat.

"I sense a Goddess!" said Harmonia.

"Persephone! You should leave now!" said Ryu.

The young Guardian vanished in a swill of fire. She was much too young for battle. All young Guardians are highly protected until they complete their training.

Ryu made sure she was completely safe but when he turned to join Troy. A massive wall of sand blocked his path. This separated them. He wondered how the Goddess had gotten so powerful. Ryu was immune to the Persephone's power but the Goddess could always find a way to break powerful Guardians such as Ryu and Troy.

"Troy!" Ryu yelled.

He needed to find Troy before things turned ugly. Everything happened so fast he could barely think of a plan to get himself out of this situation.

~***~

Troy swiftly took out his daggers holding them in a defective position; ready to attack the Goddess if she came close. There was no sign of Ryu or the women he met.

Besides fearing the original Guardian, Persephone was a thousand times more dangerous.

Troy knew the rumors that spread throughout Delos about the Goddess that captures Guardians and turns them into lethal Assassins, she can harness darkness to corrupt their divine energy and create her army. An encounter with the Goddess will be his doom to an eternal life of torture and slavery. He needed to get away from here and fast, before the Goddess could get her hands on him.

Every second that passed brought panic, for a Guardian so young, fighting the Goddess will be a losing battle. Troy searched for Ryu, tried to pick up a trail or something leading to him. He stopped the moment when he heard a growl behind him. Before he could turn around, a large beast pounced onto him. He crashed into the stone pillar. Before Troy could regain control of himself, the beast's fangs sank deep into his shoulder. The bite felt like acid as he grunted in pain. He stabbed the beast in the eye and rammed it to the ground. Troy struggled to pick himself up as the beast bounced up again but Troy held his dagger and stabbed it straight in the heart killing it instantly. He then dropped the dagger as the pain became too unbearable. The poison from the bite spreading rapidly in his blood stream. It was something he had never experienced before. Guardians have rapid healing ability but his wounds were deep and were not healing. He held onto his bleeding shoulder and realized that something wasn't right. Weakness overcame his body and he fell back onto the ground.

"Now there is a rare sight; to see a Guardian fall!" said Persephone.

Troy rolled over onto his back, he knew he was in serious trouble when he saw the Goddess. Powerless to flight back as she kneeled beside him, he slowly slipped into an unconscious state. "You are perfect for a young Guardian" She ripped opened his shirt and placed her right hand onto his bare chest. She utters a dark spell:

Let your divine light burn in the deaths of Tartarus
Bring forth your inner beast
Grant me your divine power and desire
Willingly into me

A shadow dragon appeared in the air, the sky echo with its fierce roar as it slowly faded away which meant her spell worked. She had broken the barrier of his divine power.

"Now you will be mine!" said Persephone.

Chapter 8

In his desperate search, Ryu found Troy lying motionless on the ground. Dammit Troy! Wake up!" yelled Ryu. He glanced around and there was no sign of the Goddess. He checked his shoulder and it didn't look good, it was as if some poison had infected him; slowly draining his divine energy. He turned back to see Avril approaching. "Have you seen Odeya?" asked Avril.

With his grief over Troy Ryu ignored Avril's plea for her friend who was nowhere in sight. Ryu wasted no time, he placed his hand on Troy's wounded shoulder and one on his forearm. Avril watched him closely as he worked his magic, magic that she had never seen before. She glanced back at Troy, his shirt was ripped open and there was a strange marking on his chest.

"Avril? Is that your name?" Ryu asked.

"Yes!"

"I need you to stay back, this spell will effect mortals so please if you want to live keep your distance" said Ryu. Avril obeyed his command and kept a safe distance from him. She had no choice but to trust him. Odeya was nowhere in sight. She was in an unfamiliar world and needed more information in order to find

Odeya, her fears were that the Goddess had taken her. It was clear that these people are not a threat. Ryu shut his eyes as he began to say the words of a spell.

I call upon the divine Guardians
The hidden shadow
Brutal Cerberus
The Spirit Storm
The fierce dragon
The unseen assassin
The Ancient Sea

Let your light bring life onto me.

Avril watched him closely. She wasn't sure what he was doing. Troy suddenly awakens. She could tell that he was in unbearable pain. She stood lost and confused as she watched Ryu struggled to hold him down. Some rune markings appeared around them as Troy's wounds began to heal. Avril had never seen this before, a strange world with strange people. It made her feel unwelcome.

Ryu helped Troy off the ground, "Thank You Ryu! You saved my life."

"We need to get back to the Palace, you may need some rest" said Ryu to Troy.

"No! I need to find Odeya!" Avril yelled.

Troy took out a mini pocket bag, he opened it and dropped a red dust into the palm of his hand. He throws it into the air and it formed a red crystal doorway. It was a portal.

"Wait a minute, what is that? I am new to this magic and what about Odeya? Are you just going to leave without knowing where she is?" asked Avril.

"Look! The Goddess is only looking for Guardians and your friend is not one of them so it will be safer to look for your friend in the Palace" said Ryu.

"Are you sure about this?" Avril asked.
"Trust us!" said Ryu.
"You will meet Aronzo, King of Argos! I am sure he will help." said Troy.
"Come! It's like stepping into a large mirror" said Ryu.
"Alright!" said Avril.

Avril followed Ryu into the doorway; as she passed though and it felt like stepping out of a huge bubble. As soon as Avril entered, she was captivated by the massive hall she entered. Many soldiers stood around a large shiny black table. The walls were pure black with thin silver pillars. The design was unique.

"I thought this place was empty, what is going on? why are they soldiers here?" asked Troy.

"We going to war; we going to destroy Nishikido's army!" said a strong powerful man facing them.

"You do realize you going to War, against an original guardian, you know he cannot be defeated" said Troy.

"Enough! who is this beautiful young lady?"

"This is Avril, she claims to be the Empress of Arydress." said Troy.

"I am the Empress!" Avril yelled.

"Avril! This is Aronzo, ruler of Argos and a dragon shifter" said Troy.

"It is a pleasure to meet you young Empress; welcome to my Palace, this is the war room were battles are planned." said Aronzo.

Avril paid no attention to them and walked towards the table. She glanced at a map of an unfamiliar world. Everything was strange to her but there was so much to learn. "Is this a map of Delos?" Avril asked.

"Troy! Take the Empress to the guest room, return when she is settled." said Aronzo.

"You need your rest; if she took your friend, going against Persephone won't be an easy task" said Ryu.

"Very well, I could use a bit of rest." said Avril.

"Tell the servants to send some food up to her room." said Aronzo.

Avril never thought she could trust the two strangers but she did not have a choice. She followed Troy and Ryu out of the room, not a word was spoken. They reached some stairs leading into a large passageway with many doors. Troy took her to the end, the last door. "Well! This will be your room for the night and I hope you find it comfy. It's also the warmest room in the Palace but it does get a bit cold at night." said Troy.

"Thank You!" said Avril, why, when she reached her room, she just wanted to clear her mind before she started searching for Odeya.

"Get some rest, we will meet in the morning" said Troy.

"Oh! Almost forgot. I will send the servant with a tray of food. Also some handmaidens." said Troy.

"That will be nice." said Avril.

"I will leave you now, if you need anything, please let the handmaidens know. I will be back to check on you." said Troy.

"Wait! What was Persephone after?" Avril asked.

"I have been hunted by the Goddess for years. She is taking unwilling Guardians to join her army but I am

not the only one she is targeting, she has taken many.
Ryu is here to make sure she doesn't success in
capturing me. I possess a rare power which is linked to
the Daughter of War." said Troy.

"Daughter of war? I would like to know more." said
Avril.

"Later, get some rest." said Troy.

Troy closed the doors behind him when he left. He
paused for a moment while he held onto the door
handle. He let go slowly then glanced at Ryu waiting
above the stairs. If it wasn't for Ryu he would be
Persephone's slave. He walked back up the stairs, he
was grateful to Ryu but deep inside of him. Troy
sensed that something wasn't right.

"You need more training pretty boy!" said Ryu. Troy
stood silent, all Guardians feared Erylo poison but it
seems like there is a new horror Guardians will face.
The Goddess had grown too powerful.

"So about Avril, is it true? What will you do now?" said
Ryu.

"We will deal with it in the morning. I will go and speak
with my father now." said Troy.

~***~

"Aronzo! So would you mind telling me what is going on here?" asked Troy.

"Does Nishikido know you planning to attack?" Troy asked.

"He is unaware, we managed to make plans in secret, the ships are ready to set sail in a few days maybe sooner if everything goes well." said Aronzo.

"You need to end this now, there is another war we must face, the war to stop darkness." said Troy.

"The Gods will protect us." said Aronzo.

"No! this is different, the Gods will fail and Chaos will awaken." said Troy.

"Enough Troy, I say we go to war, Nishikido's time as ruler will end." said Aronzo.

"You making a big mistake." said Troy.

Troy realized that Aronzo was very serious about war and that there was no way to stop him now. "I hope you know what you are doing, I will not be a part of this. You are on your own! This war will not end well." said Troy.

"You should be worried about Avril. The Empress of Arydress has finally come to Delos just as the Oracle predicted." said Aronzo.

"If what you say is true, then I will take my rightful place as Emperor of Arydress." said Troy.

Avril was not one that could be confined in a room, being an Empress she was also preoccupied with her Royal duties. After the meal that was brought to her, she decided to leave the room and explore the Palace.

She walked quietly up the stairs, hoping no one was aware of her presence. In the far end of the passage was an opened door. She could feel the cool breeze as she walked closer towards the door and stepped out. She could hear the eagles circling above. The garden was filled with red flowers. It reminded her of her Palace. She saw red pillars in a row near her and in the front was a large gold wall with some words written in black. The structure looked like a large passageway. The dried leaves rustled in the wind as she walked towards the wall. To her relief the writing was not Greek, she could read the words on the golden wall.

The Fall of Pallas & Divine Light

This is the untold story of Pallas
Titan of Warcraft

Pallas was handsome with his pure white hair. He also
fought with honor and strength; unlike Ares; and he
never lost a battle.

The Greeks believed that Pallas sided with Cronus in
the Great War but those were stories told by mortals,
not the Gods. The secrets were hidden and he refused
to side with Cronus or Zeus. He decided to leave the
Greek world and follow Enualios. He was intercepted
by Athena. He fought valiantly and defeated the
Goddess but although Pallas was a powerful war Titan
he could not slay Athena. He showed her mercy. There
was no honor in killing a Goddess. He gave her the
honor as his heir to rule his kingdom. He also gave her
a gift, a sword and a shield to protect her in battle.

An act of kindness coming from the war Titan came as
a shock to the Goddess. Pallas walked away never to
return.

"I thought I might find you here. I see you are
interested in Pallas!" said Aronzo as he came up
beside her; he glanced at the wall and said. "I heard

some rumours that Pallas has taken mortal form and he is here in Delos."

"I'm new to all this" said Avril.

"There are many Gods that live here, the most famous is the Goddess Artemis, she works hard to keep the peace," said Aronzo.

"I know that Goddess, Odeya talked about her when she was young." said Avril.

"Maybe if you lucky, you will meet the Goddess! Sleep well, I need to get back. I have got a war to deal with; I will see you in the morning before I head out to battle." said Aronzo.

Avril wasn't sure if he was speaking the truth. She was a long way from home and with Odeya missing it had her feel even worse but she stood calm and ready to take on any challenge. Aronzo reminded her of Atreus, a strong warrior bound by duty to protect the Empress at all cost. The history of Arydress was lost long before she was born, the soldiers were the only ones left from the first dynasty but Atreus being immortal has no memory of the first Emperor of Arydress. Avril did spend time searching for lost evidence of their existence or something that will lead back to the first rulers but there was not a single clue. She would love to know their names and what magic they possessed.

As Aronzo walked back in via the Palace doors, Avril turned towards the open fields. She suddenly had a feeling of being watched. She felt a shiver which sent chills though her body. She stood for a while, thinking of the Titan Pallas. She took an interest Titans and not just Pallas, she needed to dig deeper and find out more about the Titans and Delos.

She returned to her room in the Palace and closed the doors behind. It was the first time Avril was free from her Royal duties and it was something to look forward to after she found Odeya.

Chapter 9

Odeya awakened in a strange room in a circle of thin crystal water. She slowly picked herself from the cold floor and scanned her surrounding wondering how did you end up here. She was alone in the empty room. Persephone was the last word she heard from Ryu the rest was all a blank.

She walked across to an opened door that lead into a huge hall. There stood a gold statue of a beautiful maiden with some writing on the trident she was holding. She looked closer, she recognized the writing as Greek but she could not understand the meaning.

Ἀμφιτρίτη

The trident she was holding had silver coloured stones but they looked more like gems, it was a beautiful sight. Water flowed from her left hand but it did not touch the floor.

The dark blue pillars towered to the water roof, a thin layer of crystal water swilled downwards around the pillars and disappeared when it touched the floor.

Odeya was amazed at the sight. As she walked closer her heavy boots sank as if she was walking in water.

"Where am I?" she wondered.
She turned her attention towards the wall; clear water stretched across it. A blue curved pattern outlined the water. There was powerful magic that held the water back.

A beautiful mermaid drew herself near, Odeya placed her hands on the magical water and the mermaid mimicked her. She felt some strong energy pass through her, it felt like the power of oceans but not the raging seas, this was the calmness of the sea. "Ancient sea magic" she whispered.

Odeya watched the mermaid swim away. Mystified by this place, she glanced back towards the statue, the Greek words became fuzzy then her eye sight returned to normal and the Greek letters changed.

"Amphitrite"

She wondered if the Mermaid had transferred ancient mystical power to her. She glanced at the statue again, Amphitrite was the Goddess of Ancient Seas, the wife of Poseidon. Behind the colossal statue a watery staircase that lead onto the upper floor. Odeya became wary, wondering if the Goddess could sense her. Common sense reminded her that she does not belong here and wariness plagued her mind, she walked towards the water stairs and ran her finger into the water. As the water from her finger dripped down, the droplets moved back into the staircase. She used her hand to grab some water and dropped it onto the floor, it splattered but the water returned to the stair. "Magical" she whispered.

Odeya cautiously climbed the watery stairscase; she was relieved when she reached the top, when her foot touched a solid floor. She looked up and saw five doors in front of her. Symbols appeared on the five doors as she stared at them. One was the Greek symbol Omega.

She needed to find a way out of this Palace and the only way to do that was to push forward. She ran her finger on the engraved symbol on the first door near the stairscase. The solid black door opened. She plucked up the courage and pushed it. She slowly stepped into a massive room. It was airy and a cool breeze was blowing from the opened balcony. She still couldn't sense the presence of any other being in the room so she walked across the shiny blue marble floor to open the double doors in front of her. It was the baths. It wasn't the way out of the Palace so she closed the heavy doors. "Hello! Is anyone here?" asked Odeya a little scared.

She listened to any sound that might indicate a person but the room was silent. She decided to explore further but a strange feeling drew her to the balcony. "Sunrise" she whispered. As she stepped out into the balcony she gasped in shock when she saw a man lying on the soft chair. A surprising thought crossed her mind, how could she not sense him in the room. She glanced at him but he was asleep. He had black pants that sat low on his hips, this captured her curious mind.

She noticed a silver dragon tattoo on his left shoulder which went half across his bare chest. There were also rune markings on his hands all the way down to his forearms and on his bare chest. His hair was as black as the night sky which reminded her of someone from her childhood.

He was truly handsome and had a muscular body. Odeya had a strong temptation to touch him but she fought the urge. She slowly stepped to the edge of the balcony without waking him. She could see clouds below. It was something like a dream.

"How do I get out of this place" she whispered to herself while she enjoyed the cool breeze for a moment.

Turning towards the man, she stood frozen when his eye met hers. She didn't hear him when he stood up. When she came back to her senses she bolted towards the exit but hit a barrier and she fell violently into the floor. She forced herself up only to find him approaching. His stormy grey eyes staring back at her.

"Fylakas!" he whispered.

A strange feeling rushed through her blood. "Don't be afraid, I won't hurt you" he said. His voice was calm; which was a relief for her. "I'm lost and looking for a way out! I just want to get home, just point me to the exit and I will leave"
"I am afraid you cannot leave" he said.
"Why?" she asked.

He stood still for a moment and gazed upon her beauty but could see the worry in her beautiful eyes, he grabbed the opportunity to claim her before others do, she was a gift. Everything about her was perfect and he wanted her, to be inside her, her soft skin against his bare chest and the feel of her firm breast.

"I don't want any trouble" she said in a soft trembling voice.

Her sweet voice made him want her even more, he wanted to kiss her beautiful lips. A darkness burning within him, he loved being in control and to take want he wanted no matter what the cost, but he could sense panic in her heart, he didn't want to scare her so he lightened the mood.

"I am Nishikido! Guardian of Villadon and you are in Delos, the Greek world, home to the Demi Gods, nymphs, elementals and many more including a few mortals" he said in a deep voice. "Guardian of what?" asked Odeya in confusion.

"Guardians that battle darkness" he said.

"I see you not from Delos" said Nishikido.

"Yes Arydress" said Odeya.

"That is way beyond, tell me; how did you end up here?" he asked.

Odeya looked down in panic, she remember Arydress but it still felt like a hazy dream.

"May I ask your name?" asked Nishikido.

"Odeya" she said.

He was dangerously close to her, her back rested on the wall while his hands on either side of her blocked her path. She could smell his scent, she looked into his lusty eyes and realized what he really wanted.

Her soft hand pressed against his bare chest and she tried to push him back but he stood without moving, he was a rock "Nishikido... please don't!" she said. That didn't stop him, his finger tips stroked her hand and her markings surfaced, glowing. "What is this? asked Nishikido. "I don't remember how I got them" said Odeya.

"Rune markings on you but I sense you are more then just a Guardian. A gift or is it your curse?" said Nishikido.

"I don't understand" said Odeya.

"I should have known" said Nishikido.

He could see the confusion on her face but he did not bother to explain himself to her. She was so damn beautiful any man will desire her that is why he had to make his move fast but he couldn't take her in this Palace, he needed to return home so he grabbed hold of her shoulders before Odeya could protest. He pulled her closer, her hand pressed against his chest. She was unable to move, he was much too strong for her to fight.

Odeya suddenly felt light, as if she was floating, everything darkened, and she shut her eyes. Seconds later Nishikido let her go, he tilted her head towards his. "Sweet Goddess!" she heard him say before she passed out.

"Where are we? How did we get here?" asked Odeya as she awakened.
"This is my home, one of my rare gifts is to teleport" he said.

He gently put his arms around her and kissed her luscious lips urging her to open while he had her pinned against the wall. Waves of pleasure passed through her entire body.

Her soft moans forced him deeper into a passionate kiss, loving the taste of her sweetness. Odeya broke the kiss, resting her hands on his bare chest.

"You are going to bind yourself to me and I know you want it badly, I can feel it" he said. The word binding sent shivers down her spine but she knew that it wasn't a lie. A deep burning desire surfaced within her. His hands rested on her hips and he pulled her closer once again, she could not fight the urge to resist when he began to loosen her belt. "Soon you will be mine" he said. She stood frozen when his hands caressed her bare skin which electrified her senses.

He carried her to his bed and climbed over her, she was frozen is place, there was no stopping him. Her fear mixed with a burning desire. He captured her lips once again but was interrupted by a loud knock on the door which surprised Odeya.

"Ignore them! They will soon go away" said Nishikido.

 A minute later...

Suddenly there was knocking on the door again. The knocking grew louder, almost pounding at the door. Nishikido paused, then glanced towards the door as if he could sense something was wrong. "Just my luck!" said Nishikido.

He slid off the bed and quickly got dressed. Odeya sat up as he wrapped a silk gown around her. He gently kissed her again. "Forgive me, I promise this won't take long" said Nishikido.

Nishikido left the room without saying a word; closing the doors behind him which just killed her aroused feeling. Odeya, alone in the room, flopped back onto the bed with a feeling of being abandoned. She slid her hands down her cheeks fighting the tears. Emotions clouded her mind, she wanted him so badly it hurt deep inside.

She sat up again and scanned the room. It was large and the floor was black marble which made the room look dark. "What is wrong with me" she yelled.

She let out a breath of air and climbed off the bed and walked straight to the double doors and slowly opened it. She tried to step out but her path was blocked by an invisible shield. "oh great, now I'm trapped!" she closed the doors and headed towards the large open balcony. She was astonished to see the breathtaking view of the city, the massive buildings towering to the sky, mixed with modern and ancient designs. Some with crystal pillars. "Amazing!" she whispered.

She was truly captivated by the city and the sun's rays gave it a shiny look. She looked down, although there was a thin layer of clouds but she could not see the bottom.

"Hello!"

Odeya looked back, there stood a young woman holding a tray of food, judging by her look; Odeya could see she was a servant. "The name is Nelova and Nishikido asked me to send up some food." she said.

"Am I Nishikido's captive?" she asked.

"Captive? Oh no! The shield is for your own protection" she said.

"Protection from what?" asked Odeya.

She placed the tray onto the table "Well to be honest I'm not really a servant I'm just here to help Nishikido. Cylos and I are highly trained assassins but Delos is not our home. We are from Villadon. Home to the Guardians." said Nelova.

"I want to know more about Villadon and Nishikido" said Odeya.

"Maybe I can show you around the Palace sometime" said Nelova.

"That would be nice" said Odeya.

"I will give you some time alone, I'm sure he will be back soon" said Nelova.

Once alone Odeya started to explore the room and tried to remember something before she met Nishikido. She yawned as if she hadn't slept in days but worse of all the fuzzy feelings in her head returned. Her memory slipping away every minute until everything was a blur. She turned back to admire the breathtaking view just to clear her mind.

~***~

"Why are you here?"
"Hello Father!"
"I came her e to tell you that the deal is off!" she said.
"Iysandria, if you weren't my Daughter I will kill you with my bare hands"

"I know you have a heart, you are a Guardian!" said Iysandria.

Iysandria wanted the dagger of Helios but Nishikido, her father has protected it for centuries in Delos so he made a deal with her. He desired an Ancient Guardian Scroll which was kept hidden in the Palace of Helios and only Iysandria could gain access to the Palace ruled by a Demi God.

Iysandria realized that her father's plot was to return to his home world and then all protection from her father will vanish.

"Father?"
"You of all people should know not to stand in my way" he said.

Iysandria stormed out of the room slammed the door behind her. Her father was the most powerful and dangerous ruler in Delos, he crushed the enemies that dare to cross him. He ruled by fear so he could have better control over the land but he longed to return to the place he was born. There was another way to return home so Nishikido took countless woman to his bed in order to find a specific Guardian, one that can break his curse so he could return home without using the power of the Scroll.

Nishikido was eager to get back to Odeya but Iysandria his daughter was difficult to talk to. He had to find a way to deal with her before things turned ugly. He needed to cool down before he could get back to Odeya, thoughts of her filled his empty heart. He left the room and passed several doors, down some stairs leading into a large weapons room, it was packed with weapons, all from different origins. Rows of katana swords floated above the square pedestals.

He scanned the room for the dagger of Helios. There, at the far end of the room, stood a statue of a weeping maiden holding out her hands, her palms faced up and the dagger floated above her hands. A red shield around it for protection from enemy hands.

Without hesitation his hand penetrated the shield and he held on to the dagger. He could feel the shield pushing back as he slowly brought it out of the shield. He looked at the dagger, the blade was gold but the sun symbol was black. Three tiny spikes in the middle. He felt the blade's power but it had little effect on him. It was the only blade that can kill a God. He wrapped the dagger in a silk cloth so that it was not exposed when he left the room, if it ended up in the wrongs hands it will be the end of the Gods and he could not let that happen. He swiftly left the room and quickly climbed the stairs to his daughter's room. "You are back!" she asked in surprise.

"I will give you the dagger but on one condition..."

"I know, you don't have to tell me" said Iysandria.

"I am offering to take you and Ryu to Villadon, then you will know why I needed to leave Delos. I have been repeatedly trying to explain the truth but Ryu refuses to listen. I will show you my world. Come with me!" said Nishikido.

"After all these years now you choose to show us mercy!" Iysandria yelled.

"You and Ryu will be protected in Villadon, you have my word." said Nishikido.

As soon as her father left the room she bust out in tears. Nishikido hadn't been there as a father, Ryu and Iysandria spend their days alone. After 200 years Nishikido finally accepted them into his life but it wasn't enough to make up for the days lost.

~***~

Nishikido walked into his room, he froze when he saw rune markings in a circle around the bed where Odeya lay in a peaceful sleep. There was a small red scroll next to her, he could see the royal seal of Villadon.

He knew that she was not the one that drew the markings which could only mean one thing. Someone that he hasn't seen for centuries had appeared in the

room. It brought back a painful memory he wished
would vanish from his mind. Nishikido broke the seal
and it read:

Father
Original Guardian of Villadon

Its time for your return
Our world is crumbling without its ruler
You need to restore the Royal Bloodline
Odeya, a young Guardian is the one you been looking
for
You must claim her before its too late.

The scroll crumbled into dust, "Haruto!" he yelled. He
dropped to his knees besides the bed were she
remained asleep. After years of searching he finally
found the Guardian with a little help from Haruto, his
youngest son. Despite his son's words he couldn't just
take her by force. He wasted no time and slowly
climbed under the sheets. He wrapped his arms
around her and pulled her closer. She wiggled a bit but
remained asleep; for the first time he felt free. She
brought happiness to his bleeding heart, he never felt
this way before. He could smell the sweet lavender in
her hair. He slowly drifted off to sleep next to her,
wrapped in a tight embrace.

Chapter 10

Odeya awakened and rolled over to her side. She was facing Nishikido. He was still asleep, it didn't surprise her that he was still asleep; she knew he was tired. She glanced at the dragon tattoo on his right arm, and ran her finger down the tattoo. A smile crossed her face. "Nishikido" she whispered. He remained asleep but something deep inside her began to surface, like a beast escaping its cage. Urging her into the darkness of seduction, something that she could not control.

Odeya pulled the sheets off him and she gasp in excitement, he was totally naked. Odeya lost all control, she slipped off her silk gown and dropped it onto the floor.

She slowly climbed on top of him, her hands on his bare chest she lowered herself. Her lips met his, she gently slid her tongue into his mouth awakening him with a kiss. He opened his eyes but that did not stop her. He allowed her to take control, they break out into a passionate kiss but then he could feel the animal in him slowly taking over as his kiss became forceful.

He breaks the kiss and with one swift movement he whips her down onto her back. He climbs on top of her, "Now... I am in control!" he said, in a low seductive voice. He rested himself between her legs and looked down at her luscious body. "beautiful!" he whispered. She gave him a gentle smile, it was an invitation allowing him to take control. His rough hands caressed her firm breast. He learns down nibbling away at her sensitive nipple, sucking, rolling his tongue which brought pleasure, she trembled beneath him. He wanted to take his time to enjoy her luscious body but time was not on his side. He bite into her soft skin, drawing blood from her, she moaned in pleasure. With her blood he draws a symbol on her chest and said some words that Odeya could not understand:

Egó o ídios Déste
Ópos Párte aftí i gynaíka
Aíma tha gínei éna
I agápi as eínai mártyrás mou

I Bind Myself
As I Take This Woman
Blood Will Become One
Let Love Be My Witness

"That is unusual!" said Odeya.
"Surrender your body to me!" said Nishikido forcefully.

~***~

Odeya awaken the next morning only to find the bed empty. She reached for her silk gown and covered her naked body. Being with Nishikido had clouded her mind and further filled it with lust. She stepped out onto the balcony, the moonlight looked enchanting. There was no sign of Nishikido. She wondered if he left her there stranded; but she quickly realized that this is his home. She sat on a comfy chair waiting for his return, she didn't hear the servants enter and place the tray on the table but could smell it. Only then she realized how hungry she was. "Hope you like soup" she heard.

She turned knowing it was Nishikido. "Where have you been?" asked Odeya.

"Just taking care of some stuff" said Nishikido.

"Please sit with me!" said Odeya.

"How can I refuse such a beautiful woman" he said smiling.

He has broken his eternal curse and had claimed the most beautiful Guardian for himself and he was not willing to let her go.

The servant brought a bowl of soup for him and he took a seat. "I can take my own bowl thank you!" said Odeya. She never liked soup but when she tasted it, it was heavenly in her month and she wished for more. "Who made this?" asked Odeya.

"My personal chefs." said Nishikido.

"Personal chefs? Are you Royalty?" Odeya asked.

"Yes, you are in my Palace, I rule the Silver City. It is called Naxos, and is in Delos."

"I would like to know more about Delos." said Odeya.

"Delos is separated by two main kingdoms. I rule the northern part which is Naxos and the city of Rhodes is ruled by Neaera" said Nishikido.

"Oh! So you are Royalty" she said.

"The other kingdoms are Argos, Athens, Patras, Volos and Sparta" he said.

"Oh!" said Odeya now slightly confused.

"Argos is ruled by Aronzo, he is a dragon shifter. Athens is ruled by Cilissa. Patras is ruled by Arisbe. Volos is ruled by Isagoras and Sparta is ruled by Leicritus" continued Nishikido.

"I don't think I will remember those names immediately" said Odeya.

"But you were not born in Delos?"

"Villadon." said Nishikido.

Odeya emptied the entire bowl while listening to him. "Come! The servants brought some fresh clothes for you, it's the door to your left. I can give you some time alone." he said.

Odeya let out a breath in a sign of relief, she barely knew him and she was in a world that she knew very little about. He was there with her. His smile calmed her knowing he was strong enough to protect her.

"I see you are brave enough to trust me." he said.

"I... I know you won't hurt me." said Odeya.

She walked back into the room he directed her to, grabbed the bathrobe and entered the baths. The room had a scent of sweet lilies. The water baths had white stones floating above it. A thin layer of blue mist floating about the water. There was no crystals, nothing fancy, just a small room with only a huge bath. She slowly removed her clothes and stepped into the water, it was a perfect temperature. She tipped her head back wetting her hair. She gently rubbed the sand stone on her entire body with it slowly melting away from the heat of the water, leaving her skin soft.

She closed her eyes; the only sound was that of the water. Her body relaxed, slow breaths and waves of tranquilly enveloped her. She enjoyed the peace until she heard Nishikido enter.

"Mind if I join you?" asked Nishikido. He didn't wait for an answer and removed his bath robe and stepped in.

"I never asked you before but why were you in Amphitrite's Palace?" asked Odeya. She could see the sadness in his eyes,

"It's a story that I wouldn't want to share with anyone." he said. Odeya looked down at the shiny peal water as he moved closer to her. "I will share my story when the time is right!" said Nishikido.
"Tell me about the dragon tattoo" asked Odeya.

"Ah! you are a curious young Goddess" said Nishikido.

Her hand slid down his bare chest. She felt the hunger once again, growing deep within her. Odeya wasn't sure but something has driven her into a madness of lust. One that she could not resist.

Nishikido lifted her out of the water and carried her back onto his bed. She felt the cool sheets on her naked body, her hair still drenched but that didn't matter to her she just wanted to feel him inside her again and again. She noticed that he was much more aggressive but she did not care. She had fallen for this mysterious stranger.